TOM SWIFT AND HIS
GIANT CANNON

VICTOR APPLETON

TOM SWIFT AND HIS GIANT CANNON

CHAPTER I

ON A LIVE WIRE

"Now, see here, Mr. Swift, you may think it all a sort of dream, and imagine that I don't know what I'm talking about; but I do! If you'll consent to finance this expedition to the extent of, say, ten thousand dollars, I'll practically guarantee to give you back five times that sum."

"I don't know, Alec, I don't know," slowly responded the aged inventor. "I've heard those stories before, and in my experience nothing ever came of them. Buried treasure, and lost vessels filled with gold, are all well and good, but hunting for an opal mine on some little-heard-of island goes them one better."

"Then you don't feel like backing me up in this matter, Mr. Swift?"

"No, Alec, I can't say I do. Why, just stop and think for a minute. You're asking me to put ten thousand dollars into a company, to fit out an expedition to go to this island—somewhere down near Panama, you say it is—and try to locate the lost mine from which, some centuries ago, opals and other precious stones came. It doesn't seem reasonable."

"But I'm sure I can find the mine, Mr. Swift!" persisted Alec Peterson, who was almost as elderly a man as the one he addressed. "I have the old documents that tell how rich the mine once was, how the old Mexican rulers used to get their opals from it, and how all trace of it was lost in the last century. I have all the landmarks down pat, and I'm sure I can find it. Come on now, take a chance. Put in this ten thousand dollars. I can manage the rest. You'll get back more than five times your investment."

"If you find the mine—yes."

"I tell you I will find it! Come now, Mr. Swift," and the visitor's voice was very pleading, "you and your son Tom have made a fortune for yourselves out of your different inventions. Be generous, and lend me this ten thousand dollars."

Mr. Swift shook his head.

"I've heard you talk the same way before, Alec," he replied. "None of your schemes ever amounted to anything. You've been a fortune-hunter all your life, nearly; and what have you gotten out of it? Just a bare living."

"That's right, Mr. Swift, but I've had bad luck. I did find the lost gold mine I went after some years ago, you remember."

"Yes, only to lose it because the missing heirs turned up, and took it away from you. You could have made more at straight mining in the time you spent on that scheme."

"Yes, I suppose I could; but this is going to be a success—I feel it in my bones."

"That's what you say, every time, Alec. No, I don't believe I want to go into this thing."

"Oh, come—do! For the sake of old times. Don't you recall how you and I used to prospect together out in the gold country; how we shared our failures and successes?"

"Yes, I remember that, Alec. Mighty few successes we had, though, in those days."

"But now you've struck it rich, pardner," went on the pleader. "Help me out in this scheme—do!"

"No, Alec. I'd rather give you three or four thousand dollars for yourself, if you'd settle down to some steady work, instead of chasing all over the country after visionary fortunes. You're getting too old to do that."

"Well, it's a fact I'm no longer young. But I'm afraid I'm too old to settle down. You can't teach an old dog new tricks, pardner. This is my life, and I'll have to live it until I pass out. Well, if you won't, you won't, I suppose. By the way, where is Tom? I'd like to see him before I go back. He's a mighty fine boy."

"That's what he is!" broke in a new voice. "Bless my overshoes, but he is a smart lad! A wonderful lad, that's what! Why, bless my necktie, there isn't anything he can't invent; from a button-hook to a battleship! Wonderful boy—that's what!"

"I guess Tom's ears would burn if he could hear your praises, Mr. Damon," laughed Mr. Swift. "Don't spoil him."

"Spoil Tom Swift? You couldn't do it in a hundred years!" cried Mr. Damon, enthusiastically. "Bless my topknot! Not in a thousand years—no, sir!"

"But where is he?" asked Mr. Peterson, who was evidently unused to the extravagant manner of Mr. Damon.

"There he goes now!" exclaimed the gentleman who frequently blessed himself, some article of his apparel, or some other object. "There he goes now, flying over the house in that Humming Bird airship of his. He said he was going to try out a new magneto he'd invented, and it seems to be

4

working all right. He said he wasn't going to take much of a flight, and I guess he'll soon be back. Look at him! Isn't he a great one, though!"

"He certainly is," agreed Mr. Peterson, as he and Mr. Swift went to the window, from which Mr. Damon had caught a glimpse of the youthful Inventor in his airship. "A great lad. I wish he could come on this mine-hunt with me, though I'd never consent to go in an airship. They're too risky for an old man like me."

"They're as safe as a church when Tom Swift runs them!" declared Mr. Damon. "I'm no boy, but I'd go anywhere with Tom."

"I'm afraid you wouldn't get Tom to go with you, Alec," went on Mr. Swift, as he resumed his chair, the young inventor in his airship having passed out of sight. "He's busy on some new invention now, I believe. I think I heard him say something about a new rifle."

"Cannon it was, Mr. Swift," said Mr. Damon. "Tom has an idea that he can make the biggest cannon in the world; but it's only an idea yet."

"Well, then I guess there's no hope of my interesting him in my opal mine," said the fortune-hunter, with rather a disappointed smile. "Nor you either, Mr. Swift."

"No, Alec, I'm afraid not. As I said, I'd rather give you outright three or four thousand dollars, if you wanted it, provided that you used it for your own personal needs, and promised not to sink it in some visionary search."

Mr. Peterson shook his head.

"I'm not actually in want," he said, "and I couldn't accept a gift of money, Mr. Swift. This is a straight business proposition."

"Not much straight business in hunting for a mine that's been lost for over a century," replied the aged inventor, with a glance at Mr. Damon, who was still at the window, watching for a glimpse of Tom on his return trip in the air craft.

"If Tom would go, I'd trail along," said the odd man. "We haven't done anything worth speaking of since he used his great searchlight to detect the smugglers. But I don't believe he'll go. That mining proposition sounds good."

"It is good!" cried Mr. Peterson, with fervor, hoping he had found a new "prospect" in Mr. Damon.

"But not business-good," declared Mr. Swift, and for some time the three argued the matter, Mr. Swift continuing to shake his head.

Suddenly into the room there ran an aged colored man, much excited.

"Fo' de land sakes!" he cried. "Somebody oughter go out an' help Massa Tom!"

"Why, what's the matter, Eradicate?" asked Mr. Swift, leaping to his feet, an example followed by the other two men. "What has happened to my son?"

"I dunno, Massa Swift, but I looked up jest now, an' dere he be, in dat air-contraption ob his'n he calls de Hummin' Burd. He's ketched up fast on de balloon shed roof, an' dere he's hangin' wif sparks an' flames a-shootin' outer de airship suffin' scandalous! It's jest spittin' fire, dat's what it's a-doin', an' ef somebody don't do suffin' fo' Massa Tom mighty quick, dere ain't gwin t' be any Massa Tom; now dat's what I'se a-tellin' you!"

"Bless my shoe buttons!" gasped Mr. Damon. "Come on out, everybody! We've got to help Tom!"

"Yes!" assented Mr. Swift. "Call someone on the telephone! Get a doctor! Maybe he's shocked! Where's Koku, the giant? Maybe he can help!"

"Now doan't yo' go t' gittin' all excited-laik," objected Eradicate Sampson, the aged colored man. "Remember yo' all has got a weak heart, Massa Swift!"

"I know it; but I must save my son. Hurry!"

Mr. Swift ran from the room, followed by Mr. Damon and Mr. Peterson, while Eradicate trailed after them as fast as his tottering limbs would carry him, murmuring to himself.

"There he is!" cried Mr. Damon, as he caught sight of the young inventor in his airship, in a position of peril. Truly it was as Eradicate had said. Caught on the slope of the roof of his big balloon shed, Tom Swift was in great danger.

From his airship there shot dazzling sparks, and streamers of green and violet fire. There was a snapping, cracking sound that could be heard above the whir of the craft's propellers, for the motor was still running.

"Oh, Tom! Tom! What is it? What has happened?" cried his father.

"Keep back! Don't come too close!" yelled the young inventor, as he clung to the seat of the aeroplane, that was tilted at a dangerous angle. "Keep away!"

"What's the matter?" demanded Mr. Damon. "Bless my pocket comb—what is it?"

"A live wire!" answered Tom. "I'm caught in a live wire! The trailer attached to the wireless outfit on my airship is crossed with the wire from the power plant. There's a short circuit somewhere. Don't come too close, for it may

6

burn through any second and drop down. Then it will twist about like a snake!"

"Land ob massy!" cried Eradicate.

"What can we do to help you?" called Mr. Swift. "Shall I run and shut off the power?" for in the shop where Tom did most of his inventive work there was a powerful dynamo, and it was on one of the wires extending from it, that brought current into the house, that the craft had caught.

"Yes, shut it off if you can!" Tom shouted back. "But be careful. Don't get shocked! Wow! I got a touch of it myself that time!" and he could be seen to writhe in his seat.

"Oh, hurry! hurry! Find Koku!" cried Mr. Swift to Mr. Damon, who had started for the power house on the run.

The sparks and lances of fire seemed to increase around the young inventor. The airship could be seen to slip slowly down the sloping roof.

"Land ob massy! He am suah gwine t' fall!" yelled Eradicate.

"Oh, he'll never get that current shut off in time!" murmured Mr. Swift, as he started after Mr. Damon.

"Wait! I think I have a plan!" called Mr. Peterson. "I think I can save Tom!"

He did not waste further time in talk, but, running to a nearby shed, he got a long ladder that he saw standing under it. With this over his shoulder he retraced his steps to the balloon hangar and placed the ladder against the side. Then he started to climb up.

"What are you going to do?" yelled Tom, leaning over from his seat to watch the elderly fortune-hunter.

"I'm going to cut that wire!" was the answer.

"Don't! If you touch it you'll be shocked to death! I may be able to get out of here. So far I've only had light shocks, but the insulation is burning out of my magneto, and that will soon stop. When it does I can't run the motor, and—"

"I'm going to cut that wire!" again shouted Mr. Peterson.

"But you can't, without pliers and rubber gloves!" yelled Tom. "Keep away, I tell you!"

The man on the ladder hesitated. Evidently he had not thought of the necessity of protecting his hands by rubber covering, in order that the electricity might be made harmless. He backed down to the ground.

"I saw a pair of old gloves in the shed!" he cried. "I'll get them—they look like rubber."

"They are!" cried Tom, remembering now that he had been putting up a new wire that day, and had left his rubber gloves there. "But you haven't any pliers!" the lad went. "How can you cut wire without them? There's a pair in the shop, but—"

"Heah dey be! Heah dey be!" cried Eradicate, as he produced a heavy pair from his pocket. "I—I couldn't find de can-opener fo' Mrs. Baggert, an' I jest got yo' pliers, Massa Tom. Oh, how glad I is dat I did. Here's de pincers, Massa Peterson."

He handed them to the fortune-hunter, who came running back with the rubber gloves. Mr. Damon was no more than half way to the power house, which was quite a distance from the Swift homestead. Meanwhile Tom's airship was slipping more and more, and a thick, pungent smoke now surrounded it, coming from the burning insulation. The sparks and electrical flames were worse than ever.

"Just a moment now, and I'll have you safe!" cried the fortune-hunter, as he again mounted the ladder. Luckily the charged wire was near enough to be reached by going nearly to the top of the ladder.

Holding the pincers in his rubber-gloved hands, the old man quickly snipped the wire. There was a flash of sparks as the copper conductor was severed, and then the shower of sparks about Tom's airship ceased.

In another second he had turned on full power, the propellers whizzed with the quickness of light, and he rose in the air, off the shed roof, the live wire no longer entangling him. Then he made a short circuit of the work-shop yard, and came to the ground safely a little distance from the balloon hangar.

"Saved! Tom is saved!" cried Mr. Swift, who had seen the act of Mr. Peterson from a distance. "He saved my boy's life!"

"Thanks, Mr. Peterson!" exclaimed the young inventor, as he left his seat and walked up to the fortune-hunter. "You certainly did me a good turn then. It was touch and go! I couldn't have stayed there many seconds longer. Next time I'll know better than to fly with a wireless trailer over a live conductor," and he held out his hand to Mr. Peterson.

"I'm glad I could help you, Tom," spoke the other, warmly. "I was afraid that if you had to wait until they shut off the power it would be too late."

"It would—it would—er—I feel—I—"

8

Tom's voice trailed off into a whisper and he swayed on his feet.

"Cotch him!" cried Eradicate. "Cotch him! Massa Tom's hurt!" and only just in time did Mr. Peterson clutch the young inventor in his arms. For Tom, white of face, had fallen back in a dead faint.

CHAPTER II

"WE'LL TAKE A CHANCE!"

"Carry him into the house!" cried Mr. Swift, as he came running to where Mr. Peterson was loosening Tom's collar.

"Git a doctor!" murmured Eradicate. "Call someone on de tellifoam! Git fo' doctors!"

"We must get him into the house first," declared Mr. Damon, who, seeing that Tom was off the shed roof, had stopped mid-way to the powerhouse, and retraced his steps. "Let's carry him into the house. Bless my pocketbook! but he must have been shocked worse than he thought."

They lifted the inert form of our hero and walked toward the mansion with him, Mrs. Baggert, the housekeeper, standing in the doorway in dismay, uncertain what to do.

And while Tom is being cared for I will take just a moment to tell my new readers something more about him and his inventions, as they have been related in the previous books of this series.

The first volume was called "Tom Swift and His Motor-Cycle," and this machine was the means of his becoming acquainted with Mr. Wakefield Damon, the odd gentleman who so often blessed things. On his motor-cycle Tom had many adventures.

The lad was of an inventive mind, as was his father, and in the succeeding books of the series, which you will find named in detail elsewhere, I related how Tom got a motorboat, made an airship, and later a submarine, in all of which craft he had strenuous times and adventures.

His electric runabout was quite the fastest car on the road, and when he sent his wonderful wireless message he saved himself and others from Earthquake Island. He solved the secret of the diamond makers, and, though he lost a fine balloon in the caves of ice, he soon had another air craft—a regular sky-racer. His electric rifle saved a party from the red pygmies in Elephant Land, and in his air glider he found the platinum treasure. With his wizard camera, Tom took wonderful moving pictures, and in the volume immediately preceding this present one, called "Tom Swift and His Great Searchlight," I had the pleasure of telling you how the lad captured the smugglers who were working against Uncle Sam over the border.

Tom, as you will see, had, with the help of his father, perfected many wonderful inventions. The lad lived with his aged parent, his mother being dead, in the village of Shopton, in New York State.

10

While the house, which was presided over by the motherly Mrs. Baggert, was large, it was almost lost now amid the many buildings surrounding it, from balloon and airship hangars, to shops where varied work was carried on. For Tom did most of his labor himself, of course with men to help him at the heavier tasks. Occasionally he had to call on outside shops.

In the household, beside his father, himself and Mrs. Baggert, was Eradicate Sampson, an aged colored man-of-all-work, who said he was called "Eradicate" because he eradicated dirt. There was also Koku, a veritable giant, one of two brothers whom Tom had brought with him from Giant Land, when he escaped from captivity there, as related in the book of that name.

Mr. Damon was, with Ned Newton, Tom's chum, the warmest friend of the family, and was often at Tom's home, coming from the neighboring town of Waterford, where he lived.

Tom had been back some time now from working for the government in detecting the smugglers, but, as you may well suppose, he had not been idle. Inventing a number of small things, including useful articles for the house, was a sort of recreation for him, but his mind was busy on one great scheme, which I will tell you about in due time.

Among other things he had just perfected a new style of magneto for one of his airships. The magneto, as you know, is a sort of small dynamo, that supplies the necessary spark to the cylinder, to explode the mixture of air and gasoline vapor. He was trying out this magneto in the Humming Bird when the accident I have related in the first chapter occurred.

"There! He's coming to!" exclaimed Mrs. Baggert, as she leaned over Tom, who was stretched out on the sofa in the library. "Give him another smell of this ammonia," she went on, handing the bottle to Mr. Swift.

"No—no," faintly murmured Tom, opening his eyes. "I—I've had enough of that, if you please! I'm all right."

"Are you sure, Tom?" asked his father. "Aren't you hurt anywhere?"

"Not a bit, Dad! It was foolish of me to go off that way; but I couldn't seem to help it. It all got black in front of me, and—well, I just keeled over."

"I should say you did," spoke Mr. Peterson.

"An' ef he hadn't a-been there to cotch yo' all," put in Eradicate, "yo' all suah would hab hit de ground mighty hard."

"That's two services he did for me today," said Tom, as he managed to sit up. "Cutting that wire—well, it saved my life, that's certain."

11

"I believe you, Tom," said Mr. Swift, solemnly, and he held out his hand to his old mining partner.

"Do you need the doctor?" asked Mr. Damon, who was at the telephone. "He says he'll come right over—I can get him in Tom's electric runabout, if you say so. He's on the wire now."

"No, I don't need him," replied the young inventor. "Thank him just the same. It was only an ordinary faint, caused by the slight electrical shocks, and by getting a bit nervous, I guess. I'm all right—see," and he proved it by standing up.

"He's all right—don't come, doctor," said Mr. Damon into the telephone. "Bless my keyring!" he exclaimed, "but that was a strenuous time!"

"I've been in some tight places before," went on Tom, as he sat down in an easy chair, "and I've had any number of shocks when I've been experimenting, but this was a sort of double combination, and it sure had me guessing. But I'm feeling better every minute."

"A cup of hot tea will do you good," said motherly Mrs. Baggert, as she bustled out of the room. "I'll make it for you."

"You cut that wire as neatly as any lineman could," went on Tom, glancing from Mr. Peterson out of the window to where one of his workmen was repairing the break. "When I flew over it in my airship I never gave a thought to the trailer from my wireless outfit. The first I knew I was caught back, and then pulled down to the balloon shed roof, for I tilted the deflecting rudder by mistake."

"But, Mr. Peterson," Tom went on, "I haven't seen you in some time. Anything new on, that brings you here?" for the fortune-hunter had called at the Swift house after Tom had gone out to the shop to get his airship ready for the flight to try the magneto.

"Well, Tom, I have something rather new on," replied Mr. Peterson. "I hoped to interest your father in it, but he doesn't seem to care to take a chance. It's a lost opal mine on a little-known island in the Caribbean Sea not far from the city of Colon. I say not far—by that I mean about twenty miles. But your father doesn't want to invest, say, ten thousand dollars in it, though I can almost guarantee that he'll get five times that sum back. So, as long as he doesn't feel that he can help me out, I guess I'd better be traveling on."

"Hold on! Wait a minute. Don't be in a hurry," said Mr. Swift.

Mr. Peterson was an old friend, and when he and Mr. Swift were young men they had prospected and grub-staked together. But Mr. Swift soon gave that up to devote his time to his inventions, while Mr. Peterson became a sort of rolling stone.

He was a good man, but somewhat visionary, and a bit inclined to "take chances"—such as looking for lost treasure—rather than to devote himself to some steady employment. The result was that he led rather a precarious life, though never being actually in want.

"No, pardner," he said to Mr. Swift. "It's kind of you to ask me to stay; but this mine business has got a grip on me. I want to try it out. If you won't finance the project someone else may. I'll say good-bye, and—"

"Now just a minute," said Mr. Swift. "It's true, Alec, I had about made up my mind not to go into this thing, when this accident happened to Tom. Now you practically saved his life. You—"

"Oh, pshaw! I only acted on the spur of the moment. Anyone could have done what I did," protested the fortune-hunter.

"Oh, but you did it!" insisted Mr. Swift, "and you did it in the nick of time. Now I wouldn't for a moment think of offering you a reward for saving my son's life. But I do feel mighty friendly toward you—not that I didn't before—but I do want to help you. Alec, I will go into this business with you. We'll take a chance! I'll invest ten thousand dollars, and I'm not so awful worried about getting it back, either—though I don't believe in throwing money away."

"You won't throw it away in this case!" declared Mr. Peterson, eagerly. "I'm sure to find that mine; but it will take a little capital to work it. That's what I need—capital!"

"Well, I'll supply it to the extent of ten thousand dollars," said Mr. Swift. "Tom, what do you think of it? Am I foolish or not?"

"Not a bit of it, Dad!" cried the young man, who was now himself again. "I'm glad you took that chance, for, if you hadn't—well, I would have supplied the money myself—that's all," and he smiled at the fortune-hunter.

CHAPTER III

PLANNING A BIG GUN

"BUT, Tom, I don't see how in the world you can ever hope to make a bigger gun than that."

"I think it can be done, Ned," was the quiet answer of the young inventor. He looked up from some drawings on the table in the office of one of his shops. "Now I'll just show you—"

"Hold on, Tom. You know I have a very poor head for figures, even if I do help you out once in a while on some of your work. Skip the technical details, and give me the main facts."

The two young men—Ned Newton being Tom's special chum—were talking together over Tom's latest scheme.

It was several days after Tom's accident in the airship, when he had been saved by the prompt action of Mr. Peterson. That fortune-hunter, once he had the promise of Mr. Swift to invest in his somewhat visionary plan of locating a lost opal mine near the Panama Canal, had left the Swift homestead to arrange for fitting out the expedition of discovery. He had tried to prevail on Tom to accompany him, and, failing in that, tried to work on Mr. Damon.

"Bless my watch chain!" exclaimed that odd gentleman. "I would like to go with you first rate. But I'm so busy—so very busy—that I can't think of it. I have simply neglected all my affairs, chasing around the country with Tom Swift. But if Tom goes I—ahem! I think perhaps I could manage it—ahem!"

"I thought you were busy," laughed Tom.

"Oh, well, perhaps I could get a few weeks off. But I'm not going—no, bless my check book, I must get back to business!"

But as Mr. Damon was a retired gentleman of wealth, his "business" was more or less of a joke among his friends.

So then, a few days after the departure of Mr. Peterson, Tom and Ned sat in the former's office, discussing the young inventor's latest scheme.

"How big is the biggest gun ever made, Tom?" asked his chum. "I mean in feet, in inches, or in muzzle diameter, however they are measured."

"Well," began Tom, "of course some nation may, in secret, be making a bigger gun than any I have ever heard of. As far as I know, however, the largest one ever made for the United States was a sixteen-inch rifled cannon—that is, it was sixteen inches across at the muzzle, and I forget just

14

how long. It weighed many tons, however, and it now lies, or did a few years ago, in a ditch at the Sandy Hook proving grounds. It was a failure."

"And yet you are figuring on making a cannon with a muzzle thirty inches across—almost a yard—and fifty feet long and to weigh—"

"No one can tell exactly how much it will weigh," interrupted Tom. "And I'm not altogether certain about the muzzle measurement, nor of the length. It's sort of in the air at present. Only I don't see why a larger gun than any that has yet been made, can't be constructed."

"If anybody can invent one, you can, Tom Swift!" exclaimed Ned, admiringly.

"You flatter me!" exclaimed his chum, with a mock bow.

"But what good will it be?" went on Ned. "Making big guns doesn't help any in war, that I can see."

"Ned!" exclaimed Tom, "you don't look far enough ahead. Now here's my scheme in a nutshell. You know what Uncle Sam is doing down in his big ditch; don't you?"

"You mean digging the Panama Canal?"

Yes, the greatest engineering feat of centuries. It is going to make a big change in the whole world, and the United States is going to become—if she is not already—a world-power. Now that canal has to be protected—I mean against the possibility of war. For, though it may never come, and the chances are it never will, still it may.

"Uncle Sam has to be ready for it. There never was a more true saying than 'in time of peace prepare for war.' Preparing for war is, in my opinion, the best way not to have one.

"Once the Panama Canal is in operation, and the world-changes incidental to it have been made, if it should pass into the hands of some foreign country—as it very possibly might do—the United States would not only be the laughing-stock of the world, but she would lose the high place she holds.

"Now, then, to protect the canal, several things are necessary. Among them are big guns—cannon that can shoot a long distance—for if a foreign nation should send some of their new dreadnaughts over here—vessels with guns that can shoot many miles—where would the canal be once a bombardment was opened? It would be ruined in a day—the immense lock-gates would be destroyed. And, not only from the guns aboard ships would there be danger, but from siege cannon planted in Costa Rica, or some South American country below the canal zone.

"Now, to protect the canal against such an attack we need guns that can shoot farther, straighter and more powerfully than any at present in use, and we've got to have the most powerful explosive. In other words, we've got to beat the biggest guns that are now in existence. And I'm going to do it, Ned!"

"You are?"

"Yes, I'm going to invent a cannon that will make the longest shots on record. I'm going to make a world-beater gun; or, rather, I'm going to invent it, and have it made, for I guess it would tax this place to the limit.

"I've been thinking of this for some time, Ned. I've been puttering around inventing new magnetos, potato-parers and the like, but this is my latest hobby. The Panama Canal is a big thing—one of the biggest things in the world. We need the biggest guns in the world to protect it.

"And, listen: Uncle Sam thinks the same way. I understand that the best men in the service—at West Point, Annapolis and Sandy Hook, as well as elsewhere—are working in the interest of the United States to perfect a bigger cannon than any ever before made. In fact, one has just been constructed, and is going to be tried at the Sandy Hook proving grounds soon. I'm going to see the test if I can.

"And here's another thing. Foreign nations are trying to steal Uncle Sam's secrets. If this country gets a big cannon, some other nation will want a bigger one. It's a constant warfare. I'm going to devote my talents—such as they are—to Uncle Sam. I'm going to make the biggest cannon in the world— the one that will shoot the farthest and knock into smithereens all the other big guns. That's the only way to protect the canal. Do you understand, Ned?"

"Somewhat, Tom. Since I gave up my place in the bank, and became a sort of handy-lad for you, I know more about your work. But isn't it going to be dangerous to make a cannon like that?"

"Well, in a way, yes, Ned. But we've got to take chances, just as father did when he invested ten thousand dollars in that opal mine. He'll never see his money again."

"Don't you think so?"

"No, Ned."

"And when do you expect to start on your gun, Tom?"

"Right away. I'm making some plans now. I'm going down to Sandy Hook and witness the test of this new big cannon. You can come along, if you like."

"Well, I sure will like. When is it?"

"Oh, in about a week. I'll have to look—"

"'Scuse me, Massa Tom," broke in Eradicate, as he put his head through the half-opened office door. "'Scuse me, but dere's a express gen'men outside, wif his auto truck, an' he's got some packages fo' yo' all, marked 'dangerous—explosive—an' keep away fom de fire.' He want t' know what he all gwine t' do wif 'em, Massa Tom?"

"Do with 'em? Oh, I guess it's that new giant powder I sent for. Why, Eradicate, have him bring 'em right in here."

"Yais, sah, Massa Tom. Dat's all right; but he jest can't bring 'em in," and Eradicate looked behind him somewhat apprehensively.

"Can't bring 'em in? Why not, I'd like to know?" exclaimed Tom. "He's paid for it."

"'Scuse me, Massa Tom," said the colored man, "but dat express gen'men can't bring dem explosive powder boxes in heah, 'case as how his autermobile hab done ketched fire an' he cain't get near it nohow. Dat's why, Massa Tom!"

"Caesar's ghost!" yelled the young inventor. "The auto on fire, and that powder in it! Come on Ned!" and he made a rush for the door.

CHAPTER IV

KOKU'S BRAVE ACT

"Tom! Tom!" cried Ned, as he watched the disappearing figure of his chum. "Come back here! If there's going to be an explosion we ought to run out of the back door!"

"I'm not running away!" flashed back Tom. "I'm going to get that powder out of the auto before it goes up! If it does we'll be blown to kingdom come, back door or front door! Come on!"

"Bacon and eggs!" yelled Ned. "He's running an awful risk! But I can't let him go alone! I guess we're in for it!"

Then he, too, rushed from the office toward the front of the shop, before which, in a sort of private road, stood the blazing auto. And Ned, who had now lost sight of Tom, because of our hero having turned a corner in the corridor, heard excited shouts coming from the seat of trouble.

"If that's some new kind of powder Tom's sent for, to test for his new big gun, and it goes up," Ned said to himself, as he rushed on, "this place will be blown to smithereens. All Tom's valuable machinery and patents will be ruined!"

Ned had now reached the front door of the shop. He had a glimpse of the burning auto—a small express truck, well loaded with various packages. And, through the smoke, which from the odor must have been caused by burning gasoline, Ned could see several boxes marked in red letters:

DANGEROUS   EXPLOSIVE

KEEP AWAY FROM FIRE

"Keep away from fire!" murmured the panting lad. "If they can get any nearer fire I don't see how."

"Oh, mah golly!" gasped Eradicate, who had lumbered on behind Ned. "Oh, mah golly! Oh, good land ob massy! Look at Massa Tom!"

"I've got to help him!" cried Ned, for he saw that his chum had rushed to the rear of the auto, and was endeavoring to drag one of the powder boxes across the lowered tail-board. Tom was straining and tugging at it, but did not seem able to move the case. It was heavy, as Ned learned later, and was also held down by the weight of other express packages on top of it.

"Oh, mah golly!" cried Eradicate. "Git some watah, somebody, an' put out dat fire!"

"No—no water!" yelled Tom, who heard him. "Water will only make it worse—it'll scatter the blazing gasoline. The feed pipe from the tank must have burst. Throw on sand—sand is the only thing to use!"

"I'll git a shubble!" cried Eradicate. "I'll git a sand-shubble!" and he tottered off.

"Wait, Tom, I'll give you a hand!" cried Ned, as he saw his chum step away from the end of the auto for a moment, as a burst of flame, and choking smoke, driven by the wind, was blown almost in his face. "I'll help you!"

"We've got to be lively, then, Ned!" gasped Tom. "This is getting hotter every minute! Where's that Koku? He could yank these boxes out in a jiffy!"

And indeed a giant's strength was needed at that moment.

Ned glanced around to see if he could catch a glimpse of the big man whom Tom had brought from Giant Land, but Koku was not in sight.

"Let's have another try now, Ned!" suggested Tom, when a shift in the wind left the rear of the auto comparatively free from smoke and flame.

"You fellows had better skip!" cried the expressman, who had been throwing light packages off his vehicle from in front, where, as yet, there was no fire. "That powder'll go up in another minute. Some of the boxes are beginning to catch now!" he yelled. "Look out!"

"That's right!" shouted Tom, as he saw that the edge of one of the wooden cases containing the powder was blazing slightly. "Lively, Ned!"

Ned held back only for a second. Then, realizing that the time to act was now or never, and that even if he ran he could hardly save himself, he advanced to Tom's side. The smoke was choking and stifling them, and the flames, coming from beneath the auto truck, made them gasp for breath.

Together Tom and Ned tugged at the nearest case of powder—the one that was ablaze.

"We—we can't budge it!" panted Tom.

"It—it's caught somewhere," added Ned. "Oh, if Koku were only here!"

There was a sound behind the lads. A voice exclaimed:

"Master want shovel, so Eradicate say—here it is!"

They turned and saw a big, powerful man, with a simple, child-like face, standing calmly looking at the burning auto.

"Koku!" cried Tom. "Quick! Never mind the shovel! Get those powder boxes out of that cart before they go up! Yank 'em out! They're too much for Ned and me! Quick!"

"Oh, of a courseness I will so do!" said Koku, to whom, even yet, the English language was somewhat of a mystery. He dropped the shovel, and, heedless of the thick smoke from the burning gasoline, reached over and took hold of the nearest box. It seemed as though he pulled it from the auto truck as easily as Tom might have lifted a cork.

Then, carrying the box, which was now burning quite fiercely on one corner, over toward Tom and Ned, who had moved back, the giant asked:

"What you want of him, Master?"

"Put it down, Koku, and get out all the others! Lively, now, Koku!"

"I do," was the simple answer. The giant put the box on the grass and ran back toward the auto.

"Quick, Ned!" shouted Tom. "Throw some sand on this burning box! That will put out the fire!"

A few handfuls of earth served to extinguish the little blaze, and by this time Koku had come back with another box of powder.

"Get 'em all, Koku, get 'em all! Then we can put out the fire on the auto."

For the giant it was but child's play to carry the heavy boxes of powder, and soon he had them all removed from the truck. Then, with the danger thus narrowly averted, they all, including the expressman, turned in and began throwing sand on the fire, which now had a good hold on the body of the auto. The shovel, which Eradicate had sent by Koku, who could use more speed than could the aged colored man, came in handy.

Soon the fire was out, though not before the truck had been badly damaged, and some of its load destroyed. But, beyond a charring of some of the powder boxes, the explosive was intact.

"Whew! That was a lucky escape," murmured Tom, as he sat down on one of the boxes, and wiped the smoke and sweat from his face. "A little later and there'd only been a hole in the ground to tell what happened. Hot work; eh, Ned?"

"I guess yes, Tom."

"I thought of the powder as soon as I saw that the truck was on fire," explained the expressman; "but I didn't know what to do. I was kinder flustered, I guess. This is the second time this old truck has caught fire from a leaky gasoline pipe. I guess that will be the last—it will for me, anyhow. I'll resign if they don't give me another machine. Will you sign for your stuff?" he asked Tom, holding out the receipt book, which had escaped the flames.

"Yes, and I'm mighty glad I'm here to sign for it," replied the young inventor. "Now, Koku, I guess you can take that stuff up to the shop; but be careful where you put it."

"I do, Master," replied the giant.

"What sort of powder is that, Tom?" asked Ned a little later, when they were again back in the office, the excitement having calmed down. The expressman had gone back to town afoot, to arrange about getting another vehicle for what remained of his load. "Is it the kind they use in big guns?"

"One of the kinds," replied Tom. "I sent for several samples, and this is one. I'm going to conduct some tests to see what kind I'll need for my own big gun. But I expect I'll have to invent an explosive as well as a cannon, for I want the most powerful I can get. Want to look at some of this powder?"

"Yes, if you think it's safe."

"Oh, it's safe enough if you treat it right. I'll show you," and working carefully Tom soon had one of the boxes open. Reaching into the depths he held up a handful of something that looked like sticks of macaroni. "There it is," he said.

"That powder?" cried Ned. "That's a queer kind. I've seen the kind they use in some guns on the battleships. That powder was in hexagonal form, about two inches across, and had a hole in the centre. It was colored brown."

21

"Well, powder is made in many forms," explained Tom. "A person who has only seen black gunpowder, with its little grains, would not believe that this was one grain of the new powder."

"That macaroni stick a grain of powder?" cried Ned.

"Yes, we'll call it a grain," went on the young inventor, "just as the brown, hexagonal cube you saw was a grain. You see, Ned, the idea is to explode all the powder at once—to get instantaneous action. It must all burn up at once as soon as it is detonated, or set off.

"To do that you have to have every grain acted on at the same moment, and that could not be done if the powder was in one solid chunk, or closely packed. For that reason they make it in different shapes, so it will lie loose in the firing chamber, just as a lot of jack-straws are piled up. In fact, some of the new powder looks like jack-straws. Some, as this, for instance, looks like macaroni. Other is in cubes, and some in long strings."

As he spoke Tom struck a match and held the flames near the end of one of the "macaroni" sticks.

"Caesar's grandmother!" yelled Ned. "Are you crazy, Tom?" as he started to leap for a window.

"Don't get excited," spoke Tom, quietly. "There's no danger," and he actually set fire to the stick of queer powder, which burned like some wax taper.

"But—but—" stammered Ned.

"It is only when powder is confined that it explodes," Tom explained. "If it can burn in the open it's as harmless as water, provided you don't burn too much at once. But put it in something where the resulting gases accumulate and can't escape, and then—why, you have an explosion—that's all."

"Yes—that's all," remarked Ned, grimly, as he nervously watched the burning stick of powder. Tom let it flame for a few seconds, and then calmly blew it out.

"You know what a little puff black gunpowder gives, if you burn some openly on the ground," went on Tom; "don't you, Ned?"

"Sure, I've often done that."

"But put that same powder in a tight box, and set fire to it, and you have a bang instead of a puff. It's the same way with this powder, only it doesn't even puff, for it burns more slowly.

"An explosion, you see, is the sudden liberation at one time of the gases which result when the powder is burned. If the gases are given off gradually, and in the open, no harm is done. But put a stick like this in, say, a steel box, all closed up, save a hole for the fuse, and what do you have? An explosion. That's the principle of all guns and cannon.

"But say, Ned, I'm getting to be a regular lecturer. I didn't know I was running on so. Why didn't you stop me?"

"Because I was interested. Go on, tell me some more."

"Not now. I want to get this powder in a safe place. I'm a little nervous about it after that fire. You see if it had caught, when tightly packed in the boxes, there would have been a terrific explosion, though it does burn so harmlessly in the open air. Now let me see—"

Tom was interrupted by the postman's whistle, and a little later Eradicate came in with the mail that had been left in the box at the shop door. Tom rapidly looked over the letters.

"Here's the note I want, I think," he said, Selecting one. "Yes, this is it. 'Permission is hereby granted,' he read, 'to Thomas Swift to visit,' and so on, and so on. This is the stuff, Ned!" he cried.

"What is it?"

"A permit to visit the government proving grounds at Sandy Hook, Ned, and see 'em test that new big gun I was telling you about. Hurray! We'll go down there, and I'll see how my ideas fit in with those of the government's experts."

"Did you say 'we' would go down, Tom?"

"I sure did. You'll go with me; won't you?"

"Well, I hadn't thought very much about it, but I guess I will. When is it?"

"A week from today, and I'm going to need all that time to get ready. Now let's get busy, and we'll arrange to go to Sandy Hook. I've had trouble enough to get this permit—I guess I'll put it where it won't get lost," and he locked it in a secret drawer of his desk.

Then the lads stored the powder in a safe place, and soon were busy about several matters in the shop.

CHAPTER V

OFF TO SANDY HOOK

"What's the idea of this government test of the big gun, Tom?" asked Ned. "I got so excited about that near-explosion the other day, that I didn't think to ask you all the particulars."

"Why, the idea is to see if the gun will work, and do all that the inventor claims for it," was the answer. "They always put a new gun through more severe tests than anything it will be called on to stand in actual warfare. They want to see just how much margin of safety there is."

"Oh I see. And is this one of the guns that are to be used in fortifying the Panama Canal?"

"Well, Ned, I don't know, exactly. You see, the government isn't telling all its secrets. I assume that it is, and that's why I'm anxious to see what sort of a gun it is.

"As a matter of fact, I'm going into this thing on a sort of chance, just as dad did when he invested in Mr. Peterson's opal mine."

"Do you think anything will come of that, Tom?"

"I don't know. If we get down to Panama, after I have made my big gun, we may take a run over, and see how he is making out. But, as I said, I'm going into this big cannon business on a sort of gamble. I have heard, indirectly, that Uncle Sam intends to use a new type of gun in fortifying the Panama Canal. It's about forty-nine miles long, you know, and it will take many guns to cover the whole route, as well as to protect the two entrances."

"Not so very many if you make a gun that will shoot thirty miles," remarked Ned, with a smile.

"I'm not so sure I can do it," went on Tom. "But, even at that, quite a number of guns will be needed. For if any foreign nation, or any combination of nations, intend to get the canal away from us, they won't make the attack from one point. They'll come at us seven different ways for Sunday, and I've never heard yet of a gun that can shoot seven ways at once. That's why so many will be needed.

"But, as I said, I don't know just what type the Ordnance Department will favor, and I want to get a line. Then, even if I invent a cannon that will outshoot all the others, they may not take mine. Though if they do, and buy a number of them, I'll be more than repaid for my labor, besides having the satisfaction of helping my country."

24

"Good for you, Tom! I wish it was time to go to Sandy Hook now. I'm anxious to see that big gun. Do you know anything about it?"

"Not very much. I have heard that it is not quite as large as the old sixteen-inch rifle that they had to throw away because of some trouble, I don't know just what. It was impractical, in spite of its size and great range. But this new gun they are going to test is considerably smaller, I understand.

"It was invented by a General Waller, and is, I think, about twelve inches across at the muzzle. In spite of that comparatively small size, it fires a projectile weighing a thousand pounds, or half a ton, and takes five hundred pounds of powder. Its range, of course, no one knows yet, though I have heard it said that General Waller claims it will shoot twenty miles."

"Whew! Some shot!"

"I'm going to beat it," declared Tom, "and I want to do it without making such a monstrous gun that it will be difficult to cast it.

"You see, Ned, there is, theoretically, nothing to prevent the casting of a steel rifled cannon that would be fifty inches across at the muzzle, and making it a hundred feet long. I mean it could be done on paper—figured out and all that. But whether you would get a corresponding increase in power or range, and be able to throw a relatively larger projectile, is something no one knows, for there never has been such a gun made. Besides, the strain of the big charge of powder needed would be enormous. So I don't want merely to make a giant cannon. I want one that will do a giant's work, and still be somewhere in the middle-sized class."

"I see. Well, you'll probably get some points at Sandy Hook."

"I think so. We go day after tomorrow."

"Is Mr. Damon going?'

"I think not. If he does I'll have to get another pass, for mine only calls for two persons. I got it through a Captain Badger, a friend of mine, stationed at the Sandy Hook barracks. He doesn't have anything to do with the coast defense guns, but he got the pass to the proving grounds for me."

Tom and his chum talked for some time about the prospects for making a giant cannon, and then the young inventor, with Ned's aid, made some powder tests, using some of the explosive that had so nearly caught fire.

"It isn't just what I want," Tom decided, after he had put small quantities in little steel bombs, and exploded them, at a safe distance, and under a bank of earth, by means of an electric primer.

"Why, Tom, that powder certainly burst the bombs all to pieces," said Ned, picking up a shattered piece of steel.

"I know, but it isn't powerful enough for me. I'm going to send for samples of another kind, and if I can't get what I want I'll make my own powder. But come on now, this stuff gives me a headache. Let's take a little flight in the Humming Bird. We'll go see Mr. Damon," and soon the two lads were in the speedy little monoplane, skimming along like the birds. The fresh air soon blew away their headaches, caused by the fumes from the nitro-glycerine, which was the basis of the powder. Dynamite will often produce a headache in those who work with it.

Two days later Tom and Ned set off for Sandy Hook.

This long, neck-like strip of land on the New Jersey coast is, as most of you know, one of the principal defenses of our country.

Foreign vessels that steam into New York harbor first have to pass the line of terrible guns that, back of the earth and concrete defenses, look frowningly out to sea. It is a wonderful place.

On the Sandy Hook Bay side of the Hook there is a life-saving station. Right across, on the sea side, are the big guns. Between are the barracks where the soldiers live, and part of the land is given over to a proving ground, where many of the big guns are taken to be tested.

Tom and Ned reached New York City without incident of moment, and, after a night spent at a hotel, they went to the Battery, whence the small government steamer leaves every day for Sandy Hook. It is a trip of twenty-one miles, and as the bay was rather rough that day, Tom and Ned had a taste of a real sea voyage. But they were too experienced travelers to mind that, though some other visitors were made quite ill.

A landing was made on the bay side of the Hook, it being too rough to permit of a dock being constructed on the ocean side.

"Now we'll see what luck we have," spoke Tom, as he and Ned, inquiring the way to the proving grounds from a soldier on duty, started for them. On the way they passed some of the fortifications.

"Look at that gun!" exclaimed Ned, pointing to a big cannon which seemed to be crouched down in a sort of concrete pit. "How can they fire that, Tom? The muzzle points directly at the stone wall. Does the wall open when they want to fire?"

"No, the gun raises up, peeps over the wall, so speak, shoots out its projectile, and then crouches down again."

"Oh, you mean a disappearing gun."

"That's it, Ned. See, it works by compressed air," and Tom showed his chum how, when the gun was loaded, the projectile in place, and the breech-block screwed fast, the officer in charge of the firing squad would, on getting the range from the soldier detailed to calculate it, make the necessary adjustments, and pull the lever.

The compressed air would fill the cylinders, forcing the gun to rise on toggle-jointed arms, so that the muzzle was above the bomb-proof wall. Then it would be fired, and sink back again, out of sight of the enemy.

The boys looked at several different types of big rifled cannon, and then passed on. They could hear firing in the distance, some of the explosions shaking the ground.

"They're making some tests now," said Tom, hurrying forward.

Ned followed until, passing a sort of machine shop, the lads came to where a sentry paced up and down a concrete walk.

"Are these the proving grounds?" asked Tom. "This is the entrance to them," replied the soldier, bringing his rifle to "port," according to the regulations. "What do you want?"

"To go in and watch the gun tests," replied Tom. "I have a permit," and he held it out so the soldier could see it.

"That permit is no good here;" the sentry exclaimed.

"No good?" faltered Tom.

"No, it has to be countersigned by General Waller. And, as he's on the proving grounds now, you can't see him. He's getting ready for the test of his new cannon."

"But that's just what we want to see!" cried Tom. "We want to get in there purposely for that. Can't you send word to General Waller?"

"I can't leave my post," replied the sentry, shortly. "You'll have to come another time, when the General isn't busy. You can't get in unless he countersigns that permit."

"Then it may be too late to witness the test," objected the young inventor. "Isn't there some way I can get word to him?"

"I don't think so," replied the sentry. "And I'll have to ask you to leave this vicinity. No strangers are allowed on the proving grounds without a proper pass."

CHAPTER VI

TESTING THE WALLER GUN

Tom looked at Ned in dismay. After all their work and planning, to be thus thwarted, and by a mere technicality! As they stood there, hardly knowing what to do, the sound of a tremendous explosion came to their ears from behind the big pile of earth and concrete that formed the bomb-proof around the testing ground.

"What's that?" cried Ned, as the earth shook.

"Just trying some of the big guns," explained the sentry, who was not a bad-natured chap. He had to do his duty. "You'd better move on," he suggested. "If anything happens the government isn't responsible, you know."

"I wish there was some way of getting in there," murmured Tom.

"You can see General Waller after the test, and he will probably countersign the permit," explained the sentry.

"And we won't see the test of the gun I'm most interested in," objected Tom. "If I could only—"

He stopped as he noticed the sentry salute someone coming up from the rear. Tom and Ned turned to behold a pleasant-faced officer, who, at the sight of the young inventor, exclaimed:

"Well, well! If it isn't my old friend Tom Swift! So you got here on my permit after all?"

"Yes, Captain Badger," replied the lad, and then with a rueful face he added: "But it doesn't seem to be doing me much good. I can't get into the proving grounds."

"You can't? Why not?" and he looked sharply at the sentry.

"Very sorry, sir," spoke the man on guard, "but General Waller has left orders, Captain Badger, that no outsiders can enter the proving grounds when his new gun is being tested unless he countersigns the permits. And he's engaged just now. I'm sorry, but—"

"Oh, that's all right, Flynn," said Captain Badger. "It isn't your fault, of course. I suppose there is no rule against my going in there?" and he smiled.

"Certainly not, sir. Any officer may go in," and the guard stepped to one side.

"Let me have that pass, Tom, and wait here for me," said the Captain. "I'll see what I can do for you," and the young officer, whose acquaintance Tom

28

had made at the tests when the government was purchasing some aeroplanes for the army, hurried off.

He came back presently, and by his face the lads knew he had been successful.

"It's all right," he said with a smile. "General Waller countersigned the pass without even looking at it. He's so excited over the coming test of his gun that he hardly knows what he is doing. Come on in, boys. I'll go with you."

"Then they haven't tested his gun yet?" Asked Tom, eagerly, anxious to know whether he had missed anything.

"No, they're going to do so in about half an hour. You'll have time to look around a bit. Come on," and showing the sentinel the counter-signed pass, Captain Badger led the two youths into the proving grounds.

Tom and Ned saw so much to interest them that they did not know at which to look first. In some places officers and firing squads were testing small-calibre machine guns, which shot off a round with a noise like a string of firecrackers on the Chinese New Year's. On other barbettes larger guns were being tested, the noise being almost deafening.

"Stand on your tiptoes, and open your mouth when you see a big cannon about to be fired," advised Captain Badger, as he walked alongside the boys.

"What good does that do?" inquired Ned.

"It makes your contact with the earth as small as possible—standing on your toes," the officer explained, "and so reduces the tremor. Opening your mouth, in a measure, equalizes the changed air pressure, caused by the vacuum made when the powder explodes. In other words, you get the same sort of pressure down inside your throat, and in the tubes leading to the ear—the same pressure inside, as outside.

"Often the firing of big guns will burst the ear drums of the officers near the cannon, and this may often be prevented by opening the mouth. It's just like going through a deep tunnel, or sometimes when an elevator descends quickly from a great height. There is too much outside air pressure on the ear drums. By opening your mouth and swallowing rapidly, the pressure is nearly equaled, and you feel no discomfort."

The boys tried this when the next big gun was fired, and they found it true. They noticed quite a crowd of officers and men about a certain large barbette, and Captain Badger led them in that direction.

"Is that General Waller's gun?" asked Tom.

"That's where they are going to test it," was the answer.

Eagerly Tom and Ned pressed forward. No one of the many officers and soldiers grouped about the new cannon seemed to notice them. A tall man, who seemed very nervous and excited, was hurrying here and there, giving orders rapidly.

"How is that range now?" he asked. "Let me take a look! Are you sure the patrol vessels are far enough out? I think this projectile is going farther than any of you gentlemen have calculated."

"I believe we have correctly estimated the distance," answered someone, and the two entered into a discussion.

"That excited officer is General Waller," explained Captain Badger, in a low voice, to Tom and Ned.

"I guessed as much," replied the young inventor. Then he went closer to get a better look at the big cannon.

I say big cannon, and yet it was not the largest the government had. In fact, Tom estimated the calibre to be less than twelve inches, but the cannon was very long—much longer in proportion than guns of greater muzzle diameter. Then, too, the breech, or rear part, was very thick and heavy.

"He must be going to use a tremendous lot of powder," said Tom.

"He is," answered Captain Badger. "Some of us think he is going to use too much, but he says it is impossible to burst his gun. He wants to make a long-range record shot, and maybe he will."

"That's a new kind of breech block," commented Tom, as he watched the mechanism being operated.

"Yes, that's General Waller's patent, too. They're going to fire soon."

I might explain, briefly, for the benefit of you boys who have never seen a big, modern cannon, that it consists of a central core of cast steel. This is rifled, just as a small rifle is bored, with twisted grooves throughout its length. The grooves, or rifling, impart a twisting motion to the projectiles, and keep them in a straighter line.

After the central core is made and rifled, thick jackets of steel are "shrunk" on over the rear part of the gun. Sometimes several jackets are put on, one over the other, to make the gun stronger.

If you have ever seen a blacksmith put a tire on a wheel you will understand what I mean. The tire is heated, and this expands it, or makes it larger. It is put on hot, and when it cools it shrinks, getting smaller, and gripping the rim of the wheel in a strong embrace. That is what the jackets of steel do to the big guns.

A big rifled cannon is loaded from the rear, or breech, just as is a breech-loading shotgun or rifle. That is, the cannon is opened at the back and the projectile is put in by means of a derrick, for often the projectiles weigh a thousand pounds or more. Next comes the powder—hundreds of pounds of it—and then it is necessary to close the breech.

The breech block does this. That block is a ponderous piece of steel, quite complicated, and it swings on a hinge fastened to one side of the rear of the gun. Once it is swung back into place, it is made fast by means of screw threads, wedges or in whatever way the inventor of the gun deems best.

The breech block must be very strong, and held firmly in place, or the terrific force of the powder would blow it out, wreck the gun and kill those behind it. You see, the breech block really stands a great part of the strain. The powder is between it and the projectile, and there is a sort of warfare to see which will give way—the projectile or the block. In most cases the projectile gracefully bows, so to speak, and skips out of the muzzle of the gun, though sometimes the big breech block will be shattered.

With eager eyes Tom and Ned watched the preparations for firing the big gun. The charge of powder was hoisted out of the bomb-proof chamber below the barbette, and then the great projectile was brought up in slings. At the sight of that Tom realized that the gun was no ordinary one, for the great piece of steel was nearly three feet long, and must have weighed nearly a thousand pounds. Truly, much powder would be needed to send that on its way.

"I'm afraid, General, that you are using too much of that strong powder," Tom heard one officer say to the inventor of the gun. "It may burst the breech."

"Nonsense, Colonel Washburn. I tell you it is impossible to burst my gun—impossible, sir! I have allowed for every emergency, and calculated every strain. I have a margin of safety equal to fifty per cent."

"Very well, I hope it proves a success."

"Of course it will. It is impossible to burst my gun! Now, are we ready for the test."

The gun was rather crude in form, not having received its final polish, and it was mounted on a temporary carriage. But even with that Tom could see that it was a wonderful weapon, though he thought he would have put on another jacket toward the muzzle, to further strengthen that portion.

"I'm going to make a gun bigger than that," said Tom to Ned. He spoke rather louder than he intended, and, as it was at a moment when there was a period of silence, the words carried to General Waller, who was at that moment near Tom.

"What's that?" inquired the rather fiery-tempered officer, as he looked sharply at our hero.

"I said I was going to make a larger gun than that," repeated Tom, modestly.

"Sir! Do you know what you are saying? How did you come in here, anyhow? I thought no civilians were to be admitted today! Explain how you got here!"

Tom felt an angry flush mounting to his cheeks.

"I came in here on a pass countersigned by you," he replied.

"A pass countersigned by me? Let me it."

Tom passed it over.

"Humph, it doesn't seem to be forged," went on the pompous officer. "Who are you, anyhow?"

"Tom Swift."

"Hum!"

"General Waller, permit me to introduce Tom Swift to you," spoke Captain Badger, stepping forward, and trying not to smile. "He is one of our foremost inventors. It is his type of monoplane that the government has adopted for the coming maneuvers at Panama, you may recall, and he was very helpful to Uncle Sam in stopping that swindling on the border last year—Tom and his big searchlight. Mr. Swift, General Waller," and Captain Badger bowed as he completed the introduction.

"What's that. Tom Swift here? Let me meet him!" exclaimed an elderly officer coming through the crowd. The others parted to make way for him, as he seemed to be a person of some importance, to judge by his uniform, and the medals he wore.

"Tom Swift here!" he went on. "I want to shake hands with you, Tom! I haven't seen you since I negotiated with you for the purchase of those submarines you invented, and which have done such splendid service for the government. Tom, I'm glad to see you here today."

The face of General Waller was a study in blank amazement.

CHAPTER VII

THE IMPOSSIBLE OCCURS

There were murmurs throughout the throng about the big gun, as the officer approached Tom Swift and shook hands with him.

"What have you in mind now, Tom, that you come to Sandy Hook?" the much-medaled officer asked.

"Nothing much, Admiral," answered our hero.

"Oh, yes, you have!" returned Admiral Woodburn, head of the naval forces of Uncle Sam. "You've got some idea in your head, or you wouldn't come to see this test of my friend's gun. Well, if you can invent anything as good for coast defense, or even interior defense, as your submarines, it will be in keeping with what you have done in the past. I congratulate you, General Waller, on having Tom Swift here to give you the benefit of some of his ideas."

"I—I haven't had the pleasure of meeting Mr. Swift before," said the gun inventor, stiffly. "I did not recognize his name when I countersigned his pass."

It was plain that the greeting of Tom by Admiral Woodburn had had a marked effect in changing sentiment toward our hero. Captain Badger smiled as he noticed with what different eyes the gun inventor now regarded the lad.

"Well, if Tom Swift gives you any points about your gun, you want to adopt them," went on the Admiral. "I thought I knew something about submarines, but Tom taught me some things, too; didn't you, Tom?"

"Oh, it was just a simple matter, Admiral," said Tom, modestly. "Just that little point about the intake valves and the ballast tanks."

"But they changed the whole matter. Yes, General, you take Tom's advice—if he gives you any."

"I don't know that I will need any—as yet," replied General Waller. "I am confident my gun will be a success as it is at present constructed. Later, however, if I should decide to make any changes, I will gladly avail myself of Mr. Swift's counsel," and he bowed stiffly to Tom. "We will now proceed with the test," he went on. "Kindly send a wireless to the patrol ships that we are about to fire, and ask them to note carefully where the projectile falls."

"Very good, sir," spoke the officer in immediate charge of the matter, as he saluted. Soon from the aerials snapped the vicious sparks that told of the wireless telegraph being worked.

I might explain that near the spot where the projectile was expected to fall into the sea—about fifteen miles from Sandy Hook—several war vessels were stationed to warn shipping to give the place a wide berth. This was easy, since the big gun had been aimed at a spot outside of the steamship lanes. Aiming the rifle in a certain direction, and giving it a definite angle of inclination, made it practically certain just where the shot would fall. This is called "getting the range," and while, of course, the exact limit of fire of the new gun was not known, it had been computed as nearly as possible.

"Is everything ready now?" asked General Waller, while Tom was conversing with his friends, Captain Badger and Admiral Woodburn, Ned taking part in the conversation from time to time.

"All ready, sir," was the assurance. The inventor was plainly nervous as the crucial moment of the test approached. He went here and there upon the barbette, testing the various levers and gear wheels of the gun.

The projectile and powder had been put in, the breech-block screwed into place, the primer had been inserted, and all that remained was to press the button that would make the electrical connection, and explode the charge. This act of firing the gun had been intrusted to one of the soldiers, for General Waller and his brother officers were to retire to a bomb-proof, whence they would watch the effect of the fire, and note the course of the projectile.

"It seems to me," remarked Ned, "that the soldier who is going to fire the gun is in the most danger."

"He would be—if it exploded," spoke Tom, for his officer friends had joined their colleagues, most of whom were now walking toward the shelter. "But I think there is little danger.

"You see, the electric wires are long enough to enable him to stand some distance from the gun. And, if he likes, he can crouch behind that concrete wall of the next barbette. Still, there is some chance of an accident, for, no matter how carefully you calculate the strain of a bursting charge of powder, and how strongly you construct the breech-block to stand the strain, there is always the possibility of a flaw in the metal. So, Ned, I think we'll just go to the bomb-proof ourselves, when we see General Waller making for the same place."

"I suppose," remarked Ned, "that in actual warfare anyone who fired one of the big guns would have to stand close to it—closer than that soldier is now."

"Oh, yes—much," replied Tom, as he watched General Waller giving the last instructions to the private who was to press the button. "Only, of course, in war the guns will have been tested, and this one has not. Here he comes; I guess we'd better be moving."

General Waller, having assured himself that everything was as right as possible, had given the last word to the private and was now making his way toward the bomb-proof, within which were gathered his fellow-officers and friends.

"You had better retire from the immediate vicinity of the gun," said its inventor to Tom and Ned, as he passed them. "For, while I have absolute confidence in my cannon, and I know that it is impossible to burst it, the concussion may be unpleasant at such close range."

"Thank you," said Tom. "We are going to get in a safe place."

He could not refrain from contrasting the general's manner now with what it had been at first.

As for Ned, he could not help wondering why, if the inventor had such absolute faith in his weapon, he did not fire it himself, even at the risk of a "concussion."

How it happened was never accurately known, as the soldier declared positively—after he came out of the hospital—that he had not pressed the button. The theory was that the wires had become crossed, making a short circuit, which caused the gun to go off prematurely.

But suddenly, while Tom, Ned and General Waller were still some distance away from the bomb-proof, there was a terrific explosion. It seemed as if the very foundations of the fortifications would be shattered There was a roaring in the air—a hot burst of flame, and instantly such a vacuum was created that Tom and Ned found themselves gasping for breath.

Dazed, shaken in every bone, with their muscles sore, they picked themselves up from the ground, along which they had been blown with great force in the direction of the bomb-proof. Even as Tom struggled to his feet, intending to run to safety in fear of other explosions, he realized what had happened.

"What—what was it?" cried Ned, as he, too, arose.

"The gun burst!" yelled Tom.

He looked to the left and saw General Waller picking himself up, his uniform torn, and blood streaming from a cut on his face. At the same instant Tom was aware of the body of a man flying through the air toward a distant grass plot, and the young inventor recognized it as that of the soldier who had been detailed to fire the great cannon.

Almost instantaneously as everything happened, Tom was aware of noticing several things, as though they took place in sequence. He looked toward where the gun had stood. It was in ruins. The young inventor saw something, which he took to be the projectile, skimming across the sea waves, and he had a fleeting glimpse of the greater portion of the immense weapon itself sinking into the depths of the ocean.

Then, coming down from a great height in the air, he saw a dark object. It was another piece of the cannon that had been hurled skyward.

"Look out!" Tom yelled, instinctively, as he staggered toward the bomb-proof, Ned following.

He saw a number of officers running out to assist General Waller, who seemed too dazed to move. Many of them had torn uniforms, and not a few were bleeding from their injuries. Then the air seemed filled with a rain of small missiles—stones, dirt, gravel and pieces of metal.

CHAPTER VIII

A BIG PROBLEM

"Are you much hurt, Ned?"

Tom Swift bent anxiously over the prostrate form of his chum. A big piece of the burst gun had fallen close to Ned—so close, in fact, that Tom, who saw it as he neared the entrance to the bomb-proof, shuddered as he raced back. But there was no sign of injury on his chum.

"Are you much hurt, Ned?"

The lad's eyes opened. He seemed dazed.

"No—no, I guess not," he answered, slowly. "I—I guess I'm as much scared as hurt, Tom. It was the wind from that big piece that knocked me down. It didn't actually hit me."

"No, I should say not," put in Captain Badger, who had run out toward the two lads. "If it had hit you there wouldn't have been much of you left to tell the tale," and he nodded toward the big piece of metal Tom had seen coming down from the sky. That part of the cannon forming a portion of the breech had buried itself deep in the earth. It had landed close to Ned—so close that, as he said, the wind of it, as well as the concussion, perhaps, had thrown him with enough force to send the breath from him.

"Glad to hear that, old man!" exclaimed Tom, with a sigh of relief. "If you'd been hurt I should have blamed myself."

"That would have been foolish. I took the same chance that you did," answered Ned, as he arose, and limped off between the captain and Tom.

A great silence seemed to have followed the terrific report. And now the officers and soldiers began to recover from the stupor into which the accident had thrown them. Sentries began pouring into the proving grounds from other portions of the barracks, and an ambulance call was sent in.

General Waller's comrades had hurried out to him, and were now leading him away. He did not seem to be much hurt, though, like many others, he had received numerous cuts and scratches from bits of stone and gravel scattered by the explosion, as well as from small bits of metal that were thrown in all directions.

"Are you hurt, General?" asked Admiral Woodburn, as he put his arm about the shoulder of the inventor.

"No—that is to say, I don't think so. But what happened? Did they fire some other gun in our direction by mistake?"

37

For a moment they all hesitated. Then the Admiral said, gently:

"No, General. It was your own gun—it burst."

"My gun! My gun burst?"

"That was it. Fortunately, no one was killed."

"My gun burst! How could that happen? I drew every plan for that gun myself. I made every allowance. I tell you it was impossible for it to burst!"

"But it did burst, General," went on the Admiral. "You can see for yourself," and he turned around and waved his hand toward the barbette where the gun had been mounted. All that remained of it now was part of the temporary carriage, and a small under-portion of the muzzle. The entire breech, with the great block, had been blown into fragments, so powerful was the powder used. The projectile one watcher reported, had gone about three hundred yards over the top of the barbette and then dropped into the sea, very little of the force of the explosive having been expended on that. A large piece of the gun had also been lost in the water off shore.

"My gun burst! My gun burst!" murmured General Waller, as if unable to comprehend it. "My gun burst—it is impossible!"

"But it did," spoke Admiral Woodburn, softly. "Come, you had better see the surgeon. You may be more seriously injured than you think."

"Was anyone else hurt?" asked the inventor, listlessly. He seemed to have lost all interest, for the time being.

"No one seriously, as far as we can learn," was the answer.

"What of the man who fired the gun?" inquired the General.

"He was blown high into the air," said Tom. "I saw him."

"But he is not injured beyond some bruises," put in one of the ambulance surgeons. "We have taken him to the hospital. He fell on a pile of bags that had held concrete, and they saved him. It was a miraculous escape."

"I am glad of it," said General Waller. "It is bad enough to feel that I made some mistake, causing the gun to burst; but I would never cease to reproach myself if I felt that the man who fired it was killed, or even hurt."

His friends led him away, and Tom and Ned went over to look at what remained of the great gun. Truly, the powder, expending its force in a direction not meant for it, had done terrific havoc. Even part of the solid concrete bed of the barbette had been torn up.

An official inquiry was at once started, and, while it would take some time to complete it (for the parts of the gun remaining were to be subjected to an exhaustive test to determine the cause of the weakness), it was found that there was some defect in the wiring and battery that was used to fire the charge.

The soldier who was to press the button was sure he had not done so, as he had been ordered to wait until General Waller gave the signal from the bomb-proof. But the gun went off before its inventor reached that place of safety. Just what had caused the premature discharge could never be learned, as part of the firing apparatus had been blown to atoms.

"Well, Tom, what do you think of it?" asked Ned, who had now fully recovered from the shock. The two were about to leave the proving grounds, having seen all that they cared to.

"I don't know just what to think," was the answer. "It sure was a big explosion, and it goes to prove that, no matter how many calculations you make, when you try a new powder in a new gun you don't know what's going to happen, until after it has happened—and then it's too late. It's a big problem, Ned."

"Do you think you can solve it? Are you still going on with your plan to build the biggest cannon ever made?"

"I sure am, Ned, though I don't know that I'll make out any better than General Waller did. It's too bad his was a failure; but I think I see where he made some mistakes."

"Oh, you do; eh?" suddenly exclaimed a voice, and from a nearby parapet, where he had gone to look at one of the pieces of his gun, stepped General Waller. "So you think I made some mistakes, Tom Swift? Where, pray?"

"In making the breech. The steel jackets were of uneven thickness, making the strain unequal. Then, too, I do not think the powder was sufficiently tested. It was probably of uneven strength. That is only my opinion, sir."

"Well, you are rather young to give opinions to men who have devoted almost all their lives to the study of high explosives."

"I realize that, sir; but you asked me for my opinion. I shall hope to profit by your mistakes, too. That is one reason I wanted to see this test."

"Then you are seriously determined to make a gun that you think will rival mine."

"I am, General Waller."

"For what purpose—to sell to some foreign government?"

"No, sir!" cried Tom, with flashing eyes. "If I am successful in making a cannon that will fire the longest shots on record, I shall offer it to Uncle Sam first of all. If he does not want it, I shall not dispose of it to any foreign country!"

"Hum! Well, I don't believe you'll succeed. I intend to rebuild my gun at once, though I may make some changes in it. I am sure I shall succeed the next time. But as for you—a mere youth—to hope to rival men who have made this problem a life-study—it is preposterous, sir! Utterly preposterous!" and he uttered these words much as he had declared that it was impossible for his gun to burst, even after it was in fragments.

"Come on, Ned," said Tom, in a low voice. "We'll go back home."

CHAPTER IX

THE NEW POWDER

"Bless my cartridge belt, Tom, you don't really mean to say that stuff is powder!" exclaimed Mr. Damon.

"That's what I hope it will prove to be—and powerful powder at that."

"Why, it looks more like excelsior than anything else," went on the odd man, gingerly taking up some yellowish shreds in his fingers.

"And it will burn as harmlessly as excelsior in the open air," went on Tom. "But I hope to prove, when it is confined in a chamber, that it will be highly explosive. I'm going to make a test of it soon."

"Give me good notice, so I can get over in the next State!" exclaimed Ned Newton, with a laugh.

This was several days after our friends had returned from the disastrous gun test at Sandy Hook. Tom had at once gotten to work on the problem that confronted him—a problem of his own making—to build a giant cannon that would make the longest shots on record. And he had first turned his attention to the powder, or explosive, to be used.

"For," he said, "there is no use having a big gun unless you can fire it. And the gun I am planning will need something more powerful in the powder line than any I've ever heard of."

"Stronger than the kind General Waller used?" inquired Ned.

"Yes, but I'll make my cannon correspondingly stronger, too, so there will be no danger."

"Bless my shoe buttons!" exclaimed Mr. Damon. "You boys must have had your nerve with you to stay around Sandy Hook after that gun went up in the air."

"Oh, the danger was all over soon after it began," spoke Tom, with a smile. "But now I'm going to test some of this powder. If you want to run away, Mr. Damon, I'll have Koku take you up in one of the airships, and you'll certainly be safe a mile or so in the air," for Tom had instructed his giant servant how to run one of the simpler biplanes.

"No—no, Tom, I'll stick!" exclaimed the eccentric man. "I'll not promise not to hide behind the fence, or something like that, though, Tom; but I'll stick."

"So will I," added Ned. "How are you going to make the test, Tom?"

"I'll tell you in a minute. I want to do a little figuring first."

41

Tom had, before going to Sandy Hook, made some experiments in powder manufacturing, but they had not been very satisfactory. He had not been able to get power enough. On his return he had undertaken rather a daring innovation. He had mingled two varieties of powder, and the resulting combination would, he hoped, prove just what he wanted.

The powder was in gelatin form, being made with nitro-glycerine as a base. It looked, as Mr. Damon had said, like a bunch of excelsior, only it was yellow instead of white, and it felt not unlike pieces of dry macaroni.

"I have shredded the powder in this manner," Tom explained, "so that it will explode more evenly and quickly. I want it to burn as nearly instantaneously as possible, and I think it will in this form."

"But how are you going to tell how powerful it is unless you fire it in a cannon?" asked Ned. "And you haven't even started your big gun yet."

"Oh, I'll show you," declared Tom. "There are several ways of making a test, but I have one of my own. I am going to take a solid block of steel, of known weight—say about a hundred pounds. This I will put into a sort of square cylinder, or well, closed at the bottom somewhat like the breech of a gun. The block of steel fits so closely in the square well that no air or powder gas can pass it.

"In the bottom of this well, which may be a foot square, I will put a small charge of this new powder. On top of that will come the steel block. Then by means of electric wires I can fire the charge.

"Attached to the steel well, or chamber, will be a gauge, a pressure recorder and other apparatus. When the powder, of which I will use only a pinch, carefully weighing it, goes off, it will raise the hundred-pound weight a certain distance. This will be noted on the scale. There will also be shown the amount of pressure released in the gas given off by the powder. In that way I can make some calculations."

"How?" asked Ned, who was much interested.

"Well, for instance, if one ounce of powder raises the weight three feet, and gives a muzzle pressure of, say, five hundred pounds, I can easily compute what a thousand pounds of powder, acting on a projectile weighing two tons and a half, would do, and how far it would shoot it."

"Bless my differential gear!" cried Mr. Damon. "A projectile weighing two and a half, tons! Tom, it's impossible!"

"That's what General Waller said about his gun; but it burst, just the same," declared Ned. "Poor man, I felt sorry for him. He seemed rather put out at you, Tom."

"I guess he was—a bit—though I didn't mean anything disrespectful in what I said. But now we'll have this test. Koku, take the rest of this powder back. I'll only keep a small quantity."

The giant, who, being more active than Eradicate, had rather supplanted the aged colored man, did as he was bid, and soon Tom, with Ned and Mr. Damon to help him, was preparing for the test.

They went some distance away from any of the buildings, for, though Tom was only going to use a small quantity of the explosive, he did not just know what the result would be, and he wanted to take no chances.

"I know from personal experience what the two kinds of powder from which I made this sample will do," he said; "but it is like taking two known quantities and getting a third unknown one from them. There is an unequal force between the two samples that may make an entirely new compound."

The steel chamber that was to receive the hundred-pound steel block had been prepared in advance, as had the various gauges and registering apparatus.

"Well, I guess we'll start things moving now," went on Tom, as he looked over the things he had brought from his shops to the deserted meadow. The fact of the test had been kept a secret, so there were no spectators. "Ned, give me a hand with this block," Tom went on. "It's a little too heavy to lift alone." He was straining and tugging at the heavy piece of steel.

"Me do!" exclaimed Koku the giant, gently pushing Tom to one side. Then the big man, with one hand, raised the hundred-pound weight as easily as if it were a loaf of bread, and deposited it where Tom wanted it.

"Thanks!" exclaimed our hero, with a laugh. "I didn't make any mistake when I brought you home with me, Koku."

"Huh! I could hab lifted dat weight when I was a young feller!" exclaimed Eradicate, who was, it is needless to say, jealous of the giant.

The powder had been put in the firing chamber. The steel socket had been firmly fixed in the earth, so that if the force of the explosion was in a lateral direction, instead of straight up, no damage would result. The weight, even if it shot from the muzzle of the improvised "cannon," would only go harmlessly up in the air, and then drop back. The firing wires were so long that Tom and his friends could stand some distance away.

"Are you all ready?" cried Tom, as he looked to see that the wiring was clear.

"As ready as we ever shall be," replied Mr. Damon, who, with Ned and the others, had taken refuge behind a low hill.

"Oh, this isn't going to be much of an explosion," laughed Tom. "It won't be any worse than a Fourth of July cannon. Here she goes!"

He pressed the electric button, there was a flash, a dull, muffled report and, for a moment, something black showed at the top of the steel chamber. Then it dropped back inside again.

"Pshaw!" cried Tom, in disappointed tones. "It didn't even blow the weight out of the tube. That powder's no good! It's a failure!"

Followed by the others, the young inventor started toward the small square "cannon." Tom wanted to read the records made by the gases.

Suddenly Koku cried:

"There him be, master! There him be!" and he pointed toward a distant path that traversed the meadow.

"He? Whom do you mean?" asked Tom, startled the giant's excited manner.

"That man what come and look at Master's new powder," was the unexpected answer. "Him say he want to surprise you, and he come today, but no speak. He run away. Look—him go!" and he pointed toward a figure of distinctly military bearing hurrying along the road that led to Shopton.

CHAPTER X

SOMETHING WRONG

"Bless my buttons!" cried Mr. Damon.

"Let's chase after him!" yelled Ned.

"Koku kin run de fastest oh any oh us," put in Eradicate. "Let him go."

"Hold on—wait a minute!" exclaimed Tom. "We want to know who that man is—and why we're going to chase after him. Koku, I guess it's up to you. Something has been going on here that I don't know anything about. Explain!"

"Well, it's no use to chase after him now," said Ned. "There he goes on his motor-cycle."

As he spoke the man, who, even from a rear view, presented all the characteristics of an army man, so straight was his carriage, leaped upon a motor-cycle that he pulled from the roadside bushes, and soon disappeared in a cloud of dust.

"No, he's gone," spoke Tom, half-regretfully. "But who was he, Koku? You seemed to know him. What was he doing out here, watching my test?"

"Me tell," said the giant, simply. "Little while after Master come back from where him say big gun all go smash, man come to shop when Master out one day. Him very nice man, and him say him know you, and want to help you make big cannon. I say, 'Master no be at home.' Man say him want to give master a little present of powder for use in new cannon. Master be much pleased, man say. Make powder better. I take, and I want Master to be pleased. I put stuff what man gave me in new powder. Man go away—he laugh—he say he be here today see what happen—I tell him you go to make test today. Man say Master be much surprised. That all I know."

Silence followed Koku's statement. To Ned and Mr. Damon it was not exactly clear, but Tom better understood his giant servant's queer talk.

"Is that what you mean, Koku?" asked the young inventor, after a pause. "Did some stranger come here one day when I was out, after I had made my new powder, and did he give you some 'dope' to put in it?"

"What you mean by 'dope'?"

"I mean any sort of stuff."

"Yes, man give me something like sugar, and I sprinkle it on new powder for to surprise Master."

"Well, you've done it, all right," said Tom, grimly. "Have you any of the stuff left?"

"I put all in iron box where Master keep new powder."

"Well, then some of it must be there yet. Probably it sifted through the excelsior-like grains of my new explosive, and we'll find it on the bottom of the powder-case. But enough stuck to the strands to spoil my test. I'll just take a reading of the gauges, and then we'll make an investigation."

Tom, with Ned to help him, made notes of how far the weight had risen in the tube, and took data of other points in the experiment.

"Pshaw!" exclaimed Tom. "There wasn't much more force to my new powder, doped as it apparently has been, than to the stuff I can buy in the open market. But I'm glad I know what the trouble is, for I can remedy it. Come on back to the shop. Koku, don't you ever do anything like this again," and Tom spoke severely.

"No, Master," answered the giant, humbly.

"Did you ever see this man before, Koku?"

"No, Master."

"What kind of a fellow was he?" asked Ned.

"Oh, him got whiskers on him face, and stand very straight, like stick bending backwards. Him look like a soldier, and him blink one eye more than the other."

Tom and Ned started and looked at one another.

"That description fits General Waller," said Ned, in a low voice to his chum.

"Yes, in a way; but it would be out of the question for the General to do such a thing. Besides, the man who ran away, and escaped on his motor-cycle, was larger than General Waller."

"It was hard to tell just what size he was at the distance," spoke Ned. "It doesn't seem as though he would try to spoil your experiments, though."

"Maybe he hoped to spoil my cannon," remarked Tom, with a laugh that had no mirth in it. "My cannon that isn't cast yet. He probably misunderstood Koku's story of the test, and had no idea it was only a miniature, experimental, gun.

"This will have to be looked into. I can't have strangers prowling about here, now that I am going to get to work on a new invention. Koku, I expect you, after this, not to let strangers approach unless I give the word. Eradicate,

46

the same thing applies to you. You didn't see anything of this mysterious man; did you?"

"No, Massa 'Tom. De only s'picious man I see was mab own cousin sneakin' around mah chicken coop de odder night. I tooks mah ole shot gun, an' sa'ntered out dat way. Den in a little while dere wasn't no s'picious man any mo'."

"You didn't shoot him; did you, Rad?" cried Tom, quickly.

"No, Massa Tom—dat is, I didn't shoot on puppose laik. De gun jest natchelly went off by itself accidental-laik, an' it peppered him good an' proper."

"Why, Rad!" cried Ned. "You didn't tell us about this."

"Well, I were 'shamed ob mah cousin, so I was. Anyhow, I only had salt an' pepper in de gun—'stid ob shot. I 'spect mah cousin am pretty well seasoned now. But dat's de only s'picious folks I see, 'ceptin' maybe a peddler what wanted t' gib me a dish pan fo' a pair ob ole shoes; only I didn't hab any."

"There are altogether too many strangers coming about here," went on Tom. "It must be stopped, if I have to string charged electric wires about the shops as I once did."

They hurried back to the shop where the new powder was kept, and Tom at once investigated it. Taking the steel box from where it was stored he carefully removed the several handfuls of excelsior-like explosive. On the bottom of the box, and with some of it clinging to some of the powder threads, was a sort of white powder. It had a peculiar odor.

"Ha!" cried Tom, as soon as he saw it. "I know what that is. It's a new form of gun-cotton, very powerful. Whoever gave it to Koku to put on my powder hoped to blow to atoms any cannon in which it might be used. There's enough here to do a lot of damage."

"How is it that it didn't blow your test cylinder to bits?" asked Ned.

"For the reason that the stuff I use in my powder and this new gun-cotton neutralized one another," the young inventor explained. "One weakened the other, instead of making a stronger combination. A chemical change took place, and lucky for us it did. It was just like a man taking an over-dose of poison—it defeated itself. That's why my experiment was a failure. Now to put this stuff where it can do no harm. Is this what that man gave you, Koku?"

"That's it, Master."

47

There came a tap on the door of the private room, and instinctively everyone started. Then came the voice of Eradicate, saying:

"Dere's a army gen'men out here to see you. Massa Tom; but I ain't gwine t' let him in lessen as how you says so."

"An army gentleman!" repeated Tom.

"Yais, sah! He say he General Waller, an' he come on a motor-cycle."

"General Waller!" exclaimed Tom. "What can he want out here?"

"And on a motor-cycle, too!" added Ned. "Tom, what's going on, anyhow?"

The young inventor shook his head.

"I don't know," he replied; "but I suppose I had better see him. Here. Koku, put this powder away, and then go outside. Mr. Damon, you'll stay; won't you?"

"If you need me, Tom. Bless my finger nails! But there seems to be something wrong here."

"Show him in, Rad!" called Tom.

"Massa Gen'l Herodotus Waller!" exclaimed the colored man in pompous tones, as he opened the door for the officer, clad in khaki, whom Tom had last seen at Sandy Hook.

"Ah, how do you do, Mr. Swift!" exclaimed General Waller, extending his hand. "I got your letter inviting me to a test of your new explosive. I hope I am not too late."

Tom stared at him in amazement.

CHAPTER XI

FAILURE AND SUCCESS

"You—you got my letter!" stammered Tom, holding out his hand for a missive which the General extended. "I—I don't exactly understand. My letter?"

"Yes, certainly," went on the officer. "It was very kind of you to remember me after—well, to be perfectly frank with you, I did resent, a little, your remarks about my unfortunate gun. But I see you are of a forgiving spirit."

"But I didn't write you any letter!" exclaimed Tom, feeling more and more puzzled.

"You did not? What is this?" and the General unfolded a paper. Tom glanced over it. Plainly it was a request for the General to be present at the test on that day, and it was signed with Tom Swift's name.

But as soon as the young inventor saw it, he knew that it was a forgery.

"I never sent that letter!" he exclaimed. "Look, it is not at all like my handwriting," and he took up some papers from a near-by table and quickly compared some of his writing with that in the letter. The difference was obvious.

"Then who did send it?" asked General Waller. "If someone has been playing a joke on me it will not be well for him!" and he drew himself up pompously.

"If a joke has been played—and it certainly seems so," spoke Tom, "I had no hand in it. And did you come all the way from Sandy Hook because of this letter?"

"No, I am visiting friends in Waterford," said the officer, naming the town where Mr. Damon lived. "My cousin is Mr. Pierce Watkins."

"Bless my doorbell!" exclaimed Mr. Damon, "I know him! He lives just around the corner from me. Bless my very thumb prints!"

General Waller stared at Mr. Damon in some amazement, and resumed:

"Owing to the unfortunate accident to my gun, and to some slight injuries I sustained, I found my health somewhat impaired. I obtained a furlough, and came to visit my cousin. The doctor recommended open air exercise, and so I brought with me my motor-cycle, as I am fond of that means of locomotion."

"I used to be," murmured Mr. Damon; "but I gave it up."

"After his machine climbed a tree," Tom explained, with a smile, remembering how he had originally met Mr. Damon, and bought the damaged machine from him, as told in the first volume of this series.

"So, when I got your letter," continued the General, "I naturally jumped on my machine and came over. Now I find that it is all a hoax."

"I am very sorry, I assure you," said Tom. "We did have a sort of test today; but it was a failure, owing to the fact that someone tampered with my powder. From what you tell me, I am inclined to the belief that the same person may have sent you that letter. Let me look at it again," he requested.

Carefully he scanned it.

"I should say that was written in a sort of German hand; would you not also?" he asked of Mr. Damon.

"I would, Tom."

"A German!" exclaimed General Waller.

At the mention of the word "German" Koku, the giant, who had entered the room, to be stared at in amazement by the officer, exclaimed:

"That he, Master! That he!"

"What do you mean?" inquired Tom.

"German man give me stuff for to put in your powder. I 'member now, he talk like Hans who make our garden here; and he say 'yah' just the same like. That man German sure."

"What does this mean?" inquired the officer.

Quickly Tom told of the visit of an unknown man who had prevailed on the simple-minded giant to "dope" Tom's new powder under the impression that he was doing his master a favor. Then the flight of the spy on a motor-cycle, just as the experiment failed, was related.

"We have a German gardener," went on Tom, "and Koku now recalls that our mysterious visitor had the same sort of speech. This ought to give us a clue."

"Let me see," murmured General Waller. "In the first place your test fails—you learn, then, that your powder has been tampered with—you see a man riding away in haste after having, in all likelihood, spied on your work—your giant servant recalls the visit of a mysterious man, and, when the word 'German' is pronounced in his hearing he recalls that his visitor was of that nationality. So far so good.

"I come to this vicinity for my health. That fact, as are all such regarding officers, was doubtless published in the Army and Navy Journal, so it might easily become known to almost anyone. I receive a letter which I think is from Tom Swift, asking me to attend the test. As the distance is short I go, only to find that the letter has been forged, presumably by a German.

"Question: Can the same German be the agent in both cases?"

"Bless my arithmetic! how concisely you put it!" exclaimed Mr. Damon.

"It is part of my training, I suppose," remarked the officer. "But it strikes me that if we find your German spy, Tom, we will find the man who played the joke on me. And if I do find him—well, I think I shall know how to deal with him," and General Waller assumed his characteristic haughty attitude.

"I believe you are right, General," spoke Tom. "Though why any German would want to prevent my experiments, or even damage my property, and possibly injure my friends, I cannot understand."

"Nor can I," spoke the officer.

"I am sorry you have had your trouble for nothing," went on Tom. "And, if you are in this vicinity when I conduct my next test, I shall be glad to have you come. I will send word by Mr. Damon, and then there will be no chance of a mistake."

"Thank you, Tom, I shall be glad to come. I do not know how long I shall remain in this vicinity. If I knew where to look for the German I would make a careful search. As it is, I shall turn this letter over to the United States Secret Service, and see what its agents can do. And, Tom, if you are annoyed again, let me know. You are a sort of rival, so to speak, but, after all, we are both working to serve Uncle Sam. I'll do my best to protect you."

"Thank you, sir," replied Tom. "On my part, I shall keep a good lookout. It will be a bold spy who gets near my shop after this. I'm going to put up my highly-charged protecting electric wires again. We were just talking about them when you came in. Would you like to look about here, General?"

"I would, indeed, Tom. Have you made your big gun yet?"

"No, but I am working on the plans. I want first to decide on the kind of explosive I am to use, so I can make my gun strong enough to stand it."

"A wise idea. I think there is where I made my mistake. I did not figure carefully enough on the strength of material. The internal pressure of the powder I used, as well as the muzzle velocity of my projectile, were both greater than they should have been. Take a lesson from my failure. But I am going to start on another gun soon, and—Tom Swift—I am going to try to beat you!"

"All right, General," answered Tom, genially. "May the best gun win!"

"Bless my powder box!" cried Mr. Damon. "That's the way to talk."

General Waller was much interested in going about Tom's shop, and expressed his surprise at the many inventions he saw. While ordnance matters, big guns and high explosives were his hobby, nevertheless the airships were a source of wonder to him.

"How do you do it, Tom?" he asked.

"Oh, by keeping at it," was the modest answer. "Then my good friends here— Ned and Mr. Damon—help me."

"Bless my check book!" exclaimed the odd gentleman. "It is very little help I give, Tom."

General Waller soon took his departure, promising to call again, to see Tom's test if one were held. He also repeated his determination to set the Secret Service men at work to discover the mysterious German.

"I can't imagine who would want to injure you or me, Tom Swift," he said.

"Do you think they wanted to injure you, General?" asked Mr. Damon.

"It would seem so," remarked Ned. "That man doped Tom's powder, hoping to make it so powerful that it would blow up everything. Then he sends word to the General to be present. If there had been a blow-up he would have gone with it."

"Bless my gaiters, yes!" exclaimed Mr. Damon.

"Well, we'll see if we can ferret him out!" spoke the officer as he took his leave.

Tom, Ned and the others talked the matter over at some length.

"I wonder if we could trace that man who rode away on the motor-cycle?" said Ned.

"We'll try," decided Tom, energetically, and in the electric runabout, that had once performed such a service to his father's bank, the young inventor and his chum were soon traversing the road taken by the spy. They got some traces of him—that is, several persons had seen him pass—but that was all. So they had to record one failure at least.

"I wonder if the General himself could have sent that letter?" mused Ned, as they returned home.

"What! To himself?" cried Tom, in amazement.

"He might have," went on Ned, coolly. "You see, Tom, he admits that he was jealous of you. Now what is there to prevent him from hiring someone to dope your powder, and then, to divert suspicion from himself, faking up a letter and inviting himself to the blowout."

"But if he did that—which I don't believe—why would he come when there was danger, in case his trick worked, of the whole place being blown to kingdom come."

"Ah, but you notice he didn't arrive until after danger of an explosion had passed," commented Ned.

"Oh, pshaw!" cried Tom. "I don't take any stock in that theory."

"Well, maybe not," replied Ned. "But it's worth thinking about. I believe if General Waller could prevent you from inventing your big gun, he would."

The days that followed were busy ones for Tom. He worked on the powder problem from morning to night, scoring many failures and only a few successes. But he did not give up, and in the meanwhile drew tentative plans for the big gun.

One evening, after a hard day's work, he went to the library where his father was reading.

"Tom," said Mr. Swift, "do you remember that old fortune hunter, Alec Peterson, who wanted me to go into that opal mine scheme?"

"Yes, Dad. What about him? Has he found it?"

"No, he writes to say he reached the island safely, and has been working some time. He hasn't had any success yet in locating the mine; but he hopes to find it in a week or so."

"That's just like him," murmured Tom. "Well, Dad, if you lose the ten thousand dollars I guess I'll have to make it up to you, for it was on my account that you made the investment."

"Well, you're worth it, Tom," replied his father, with a smile.

CHAPTER XII

A POWERFUL BLAST

"Look out with that box, Koku! Handle it as though it contained a dozen eggs of the extinct great auk, worth about a thousand dollars apiece.

"Eradicate! Don't you dare stumble while you're carrying that tube. If you do, you'll never do it again!"

"By golly, Massa Tom! I—I's gwine t' walk on mah tiptoes all de way!"

Thus Eradicate answered the young inventor, while the giant, Koku, who was carrying a heavy case, nodded his head to show that he understood the danger of his task.

"So you think you've got the right stuff this time, Tom?" asked Ned Newton.

"I'm allowing myself to hope so, Ned."

"Bless my woodpile!" cried Mr. Damon. "I—I really think I'm getting nervous."

It was one afternoon, about two weeks after Tom had made his first test of the new powder. Now, after much hard work, and following many other tests, some of which were more or less successful, he had reached the point where he believed he was on the threshold of success. He had succeeded in making a new explosive that, in the preliminary tests, in which only a small quantity was used, gave promise of being more powerful than any Tom had ever experimented with—his own or the product of some other inventor.

And his experiments had not always been harmless. Once he came within a narrow margin of blowing up the shop and himself with it, and on another occasion some of the slow-burning powder, failing to explode, had set ablaze a shack in which he was working.

Only for the prompt action of Koku, Tom might have been seriously injured. As it was he lost some valuable patterns and papers.

But he had gone on his way, surmounting failure after failure, until now he was ready for the supreme test. This was to be the explosion of a large quantity of the powder in a specially prepared steel tube of great thickness. It was like a miniature cannon, but, unlike the first small one, where the test had failed, this one would carry a special projectile, that would be aimed at an armor plate set up on a big hill.

Tom's hope was that this big blast would show such pressure in foot-tons, and give such muzzle velocity to the projectile, and at the same time such penetrating power, that he would be justified in taking it as the basis of his explosive, and using it in the big gun he intended to make.

The preliminaries had been completed. The special steel tube had been constructed, and mounted on a heavy carriage in a distant part of the Swift grounds. A section of armor plate, a foot and a half in thickness, had been set up at the proper distance. A new projectile, with a hard, penetrating point, had been made—a sort of miniature of the one Tom hoped to use in his giant cannon.

Now the young inventor and his friends were on their way to the scene of the test, taking the powder and other necessaries, including the primers, with them. Tom, Ned and Mr. Damon had some of the gauges to register the energy expended by the improvised cannon. There were charts to be filled in, and other details to be looked after.

"So General Waller won't be here?" remarked Ned, as they walked along, Tom keeping a watchful eye on Koku.

"No," was the reply. "He has gone back to Sandy Hook. He wrote that his health was better, and that he wanted to resume work on a new type of gun."

"I guess he's afraid you'll beat him out, Tom," laughed Ned. "You take my advice, and look out for General Waller."

"Nonsense! I say, Rad! Look out with those primers!"

"I'se lookin' out, Massa Tom. Golly, I don't laik dis yeah job at all! I—I guess I'd better be gittin' at dat whitewashin', Massa Tom. Dat back fence suah needs a coat mighty bad."

"Never you mind about the whitewashing, Rad. You just stick around here for a while. I may need you to sit on the cannon to hold it down."

"Sit on a cannon, Massa Tom! Say, looky heah now! You jest take dese primary things from dish yeah coon. I—I'se got t' go!"

"Why, what's the matter, Rad? Surely you're not afraid; are you?" and Tom winked at Ned.

"No, Massa Tom, I'se not prezactly 'skeered, but I done jest 'membered dat I didn't gib mah mule Boomerang any oats t'day, an' he's suahly gwine t' be desprit mad at me fo' forgettin' dat. I—I'd better go!"

"Nonsense, Rad! I was only fooling. You can go as soon as we get to my private proving grounds, if you like. But you'll have to carry those primers, for all the rest of us have our hands full. Only be careful of 'em!"

"I—I will, Massa Tom."

They kept on, and it was noticed that Mr. Damon gave nervous glances from time to time in the direction of Koku, who was carrying the box of powder. The giant himself, however, did not seem to know the meaning of fear. He carried the box, which contained enough explosive to blow them all into fragments, with as much composure as though it contained loaves of bread.

"Now you can go, Rad," announced Tom, when they reached the lonely field where, pointing toward a big hill, was the little cannon.

"Good, Massa Tom!" cried the colored man, and from the way in which he hurried off no one would ever suspect him of having rheumatic joints.

"Say, that stuff looks just like Swiss cheese," remarked Ned, as Tom opened the box of explosive. It would be incorrect to call it powder, for it had no more the appearance of gunpowder, or any other "powder," than, as Ned said, swiss cheese.

And, indeed, the powerful stuff bore a decided resemblance to that peculiar product of the dairy. It was in thin sheets, with holes pierced through it here and there, irregularly.

"The idea is," Tom explained, "to make a quick-burning explosive. I want the concussion to be scattered through it all at once. It is set off by concussion, you see," he went on. "A sort of cartridge is buried in the middle of it, after it has been inserted in the cannon breech. The cartridge is exploded by a primer, which responds to an electric current. The thin plates, with holes corresponding to the centre hole in a big grain of the hexagonal powder, will, I hope, cause the stuff to burn quickly, and give a tremendous pressure. Now we'll put some in the steel tube, and see what happens."

Even Tom was a little nervous as he prepared for this latest test. But he was not nervous enough to drop any of those queer, cheese-like slabs. For, though he knew that a considerable percussion was needed to set them off, it would not do to take chances. High explosives do not always act alike, even under the same given conditions. What might with perfect safety be done at one time, could not be repeated at another. Tom knew this, and was very careful.

The powder, as I shall occasionally call it for the sake of convenience, though it was not such in the strict sense of the word—the powder was put in the small cannon, together with the primer. Then the wires were attached to it, and extended off for some distance.

"But we won't attach the battery until the last moment," Tom said. "I don't want a premature explosion."

The projectile was also put in, and Tom once more looked to see that the armor plate was in place. Then he adjusted the various gauges to get readings of the power and energy created by his new explosive.

"Well, I guess we're all ready," he announced to his friends. "I'll hook on the battery now, and we'll get off behind that other hill. I had Koku make a sort of cave there—a miniature bomb-proof, that will shelter us."

"Do you think the blast will be powerful enough to make it necessary?" asked Mr. Damon.

"It will, if this larger quantity of explosive acts anything like the small samples I set off," replied the young inventor.

The electric wires were carried behind the protecting hill, whither they all retired.

"Here she goes!" exclaimed Tom, after a pause.

His thumb pressed the electric button, and instantly the ground shook with the tremor of a mighty blast, while a deafening sound reared about them. The earth trembled, and there was a big sheet of flame, seen even in the powerful sunlight.

"Something happened, anyhow!" yelled Tom above the reverberating echoes.

CHAPTER XIII

CASTING THE CANNON

"Come on!" yelled Ned. "We'll see how this experiment came out!" and he started to run from beneath the shelter of the hill.

"Hold on!" shouted Tom, laying a restraining hand on his chum's shoulder.

"Why, what's the matter?" asked Ned in surprise.

"Some of that powder may not have exploded," went on the young inventor. "From the sound made I should say the gun burst, and, if it did, that gelatin is bound to be scattered about. There may be a mass of it burning loose somewhere, and it may go off. It ought not to, if my theory about it being harmless in the open is correct, but the trouble is that it's only a theory. Wait a few seconds."

Anxiously they lingered, the echoes of the blast still in their ears, and a peculiar smell in their nostrils.

"But there's no smoke," said Mr. Damon. "Bless my spyglass! I always thought there was smoke at an explosion."

"This is a sort of smokeless powder," explained Tom. "It throws off a slight vapor when it is ignited, but not much. I guess it's safe to go out now. Come on!"

He dropped the pushbutton connected with the igniting battery, and, followed by the others, raced to the scene of the experiment. A curious sight met their eyes.

A great hole had been torn in the hillside, and another where the improvised gun had stood. The gun itself seemed to have disappeared.

"Why—why—where is it?" asked Ned.

"Burst to pieces I guess," replied Tom. "I was afraid that charge was a bit too heavy."

"No, here it is!" shouted Mr. Damon, circling off to one side. "It's been torn from the carriage, and partly buried in the ground," and he indicated a third excavation in the earth.

It was as he had said. The terrific blast had sheared the gun from its temporary carriage, thrown it into the air, and it had come down to bury itself in the soft ground. The carriage had torn loose from the concrete base, and was tossed off in another direction.

"Is the gun shattered?" asked Tom, anxious to know how the weapon had fared. It was, in a sense, a sort of small model of the giant cannon he intended to have cast.

"The breech is cracked a little," answered Mr. Damon, who was examining it; "but otherwise it doesn't seem to be much damaged."

"Good," cried Tom. "Another steel jacket will remedy that defect. I guess I'm on the right road at last. But now to see what became of that armor plate."

"Dinner plate not here," spoke Koku, who could not understand how there could be two kind of plates in the world. "Dinner plate gone, but big hole here, and he indicated one in the side of the hill.

"I expect that is where the armor plate is," said Tom, trying not to laugh at the mistake of his giant servant. "Take a look in there, Koku, and, if you can get hold of it, pull it out for us. I'm afraid the piece of nickel-steel armor proved too much for my projectile. But we'll have a look."

Koku disappeared into the miniature cave that had been torn in the side of the bill. It was barely large enough to allow him to go in. But Tom knew none other of them could hope to loosen the piece of steel, imbedded as it must be in the solid earth.

Presently they heard Koku grunting and groaning. He seemed to be having quite a struggle.

"Can you get it, Koku?" asked Tom. "Or shall I send for picks and shovels."

"Me get, Master," was the muffled answer.

Then came a shout, as though in anger Koku had dared the buried plate to defy him. There was a shower of earth at the mouth of the cave, and the giant staggered out with the heavy piece of armor plate. At the sight of it Tom uttered a cry.

"Look!" he shouted. "My projectile went part way through and then carried the plate with it into the side of the hill. Talk about a powerful explosive! I've struck it, all right!"

It was as he had said. The projectile, driven with almost irresistible force, had bitten its way through the armor plate, but a projection at the base of the shell had prevented it from completely passing through. Then, with the energy almost unabated, the projectile had torn the plate loose and hurled it, together with its own body, into the solid earth of the hillside. There, as Koku held them up, they could all see the shell imbedded in the plate, the point sticking out on the other side, as a boy might spear an apple with a sharp stick.

"Bless my spectacle case!" cried Mr. Damon. "This is the greatest ever!"

"It sure is," agreed Ned. "Tom, my boy, I guess you can now make the longest shots on record."

"I can as soon as I get my giant cannon, perhaps," admitted the young inventor. "I think I have solved the problem of the explosive. Now to work on the cannon."

An examination of the gauges, which, being attached to the cannon and plate by electric wires, were not damaged when the blast came, showed that Tom's wildest hopes had been confirmed. He had the most powerful explosive ever made—or at least as far as he had any knowledge, and he had had samples of all the best makes.

Concerning Tom's powder, or explosive, I will only say that he kept the formula of it secret from all save his father. All that he would admit, when the government experts asked him about it, later, was that the base was not nitro-glycerine, but that this entered into it. He agreed, however, in case his gun was accepted by the government, to disclose the secret to the ordnance officers.

But Tom's work was only half done. It was one thing to have a powerful explosive, but there must be some means of utilizing it safely—some cannon in which it could be fired to send a projectile farther than any cannon had ever sent one. And to do this much work was necessary.

Tom figured and planned, far into the night, for many weeks after that. He had to begin all over again, working from the basis of the power of his new explosive. And he had many new problems to figure out.

But finally he had constructed—on paper—a gun that was to his liking. The most exhaustive figuring proved that it had a margin of safety that would obviate all danger of its bursting, even with an accidental over-charge.

"And the next thing is to get the gun cast," said Tom to Ned one day.

"Are you going to do it in your shops?" his chum asked.

"No; it would be out of the question for me. I haven't the facilities. I'm going to give the contract to the Universal Steel Company. We'll pay them a visit in a day or two."

But even the great facilities of the steel corporation proved almost inadequate for Tom's giant cannon. When he showed the drawings, on which he had already secured a patent, the manager balked.

"We can't cast that gun here!" he said.

"Oh, yes, you can!" declared Tom, who had inspected the plant. "I'll show you how."

"Why, we haven't a mould big enough for the central core," was another objection.

"Then we'll make one," declared Tom "We'll dig a pit in the earth, and after it is properly lined we can make the cast there."

"I never thought of that!" exclaimed the manager. "Perhaps it can be done."

"Of course it can!" cried Tom. "Do you think you can shrink on the jackets, and rifle the central tube?"

"Oh, yes, we can do that. The initial cast was what stumped me. But we'll go ahead now."

"And you can wind the breech with wire, and braze it on; can't you?" persisted Tom.

"Yes, I think so. Are you going to have a wire-wound gun?"

"That, in combination with a steel-jacketed one. I'm going to take no chances with 'Swiftite'!" laughed Tom, for so he had named his new explosive, in honor of his father, who had helped him with the formula.

"It must be mighty powerful," exclaimed the manager.

"It is," said Tom, simply.

I am not going to tire my readers with the details leading up to the casting of Tom's big cannon. Sufficient to say that the general plan, in brief, was this: A hole would be dug in the earth, in the center of the largest casting shop—a hole as deep as the gun was to be long. This was about one hundred feet, though the gun, when finished, would be somewhat shorter than this. An allowance was to be made for cutting.

In the center of this hole would be a small "core" made of asbestos and concrete mixed. Around this would be poured the molten steel from great caldrons. It would flow into the hole. The sides of earth—lined with fire-clay—would hold it in, and the middle core would make a hole throughout the length of the central part of the gun. Afterward this hole would be bored and rifled to the proper calibre.

After this central part was done, steel jackets or sleeves would be put on, red-hot, and allowed to shrink. Then would come a winding of wire, to further strengthen the tube, and then more sleeves or jackets. In this way the gun would be made very strong.

As the greatest pressure would come at the breech, or in the powder chamber there, the gun would be thickest at this point, decreasing in size to the muzzle.

It took many weary weeks to get ready for the first cast, but finally Tom received word that it was to be made, and with Ned, and Mr. Damon, he proceeded to the plant of the steel concern.

There was some delay, but finally the manager gave the word. Tom and his friends, standing on a high gallery, watched the tapping of the combined furnaces that were to let the molten steel into the caldrons. There were several of these, and their melted contents were to be poured into the mould at the same time.

Out gushed the liquid steel, giving off a myriad of sparks. The workers, as well as the visitors, had to wear violet-tinted glasses to protect their eyes from the glare.

"Hoist away!" cried the manager, and the electric cranes started off with the caldrons of liquid fire, weighing many tons.

"Pour!" came the command, and into the pit in the earth splashed the melted steel that was to form the big cannon. From each caldron there issued a stream of liquid metal of intense heat. There were numerous explosions as the air bubbles burst—explosions almost like a battery in action.

"So far so good!" exclaimed the manager, with a sigh of relief as the last of the melted stuff ran into the mould. "Now, when it cools, which won't be for some days, we'll see what we have."

"I hope it contains no flaws," spoke Tom, "That is the worst of big guns—you never can tell when a flaw will develop. But I hope—"

Tom was interrupted by the sound of a dispute at one of the outer doors of the shop.

"But I tell you I must go in—I belong here in!" a voice cried. It had a German accent, and at the sound of it Tom and Ned looked at each other.

"Who is there?" asked the manager sharply of the foreman..

"Oh, a crazy German. He belongs in one of the other shops, and I guess he's mixed up. He thinks he belongs here. I sent him about his business."

"That is right," remarked the manager. "I gave orders, at your request," he said to Tom, "that no one but the men in this part of the plant were to be present at the casting. I can't understand what that fellow wanted."

CHAPTER XIV

A NIGHT INTRUDER

"Tom, aren't you going to try to get a look at that German?" whispered Ned, as he and his chum came down from the elevated gallery at the conclusion of the cast. "I mean the one who tried to get in!"

"I'd like to, Ned, but I don't want to arouse any suspicion," replied Tom. "I've got to stay here a while yet, and arrange about shrinking on the jackets, after the core is rifled. I don't see how—"

"I'll slip out and see if I can get a peep at him," went on Ned. "If it's like the one Koku described, we'll know that he's still after you."

"All right, Ned. Do as you like, only be cautious."

"I will," promised Tom's chum. So, while the young inventor was busy arranging details with the steel manager, Ned slipped out of a side door of the casting shop, and looked about the yard. He saw a little group of workmen surrounding a man who appeared to be angry.

"I dell you dot is my shop!" one of the men was heard to exclaim—a man whom the others appeared to dragging away with main force.

"And I tell you, Baudermann, that you're mistaken!" insisted one, evidently a foreman. "I told you to work in the brazing department. What do you want to try to force your way into the heavy casting department for? Especially when we're doing one of the biggest jobs that we ever handled—making the new Swift cannon."

"Oh, iss dot vot vas going on in dere?" asked the man addressed as Baudermann. "Shure den, I makes a misdake. I ask your pardon, Herr Blackwell. I to mine own apartment will go. But I dinks my foreman sends me to dot place," and he indicated the casting shop from which he had just been barred.

"All right!" exclaimed the foreman. "Don't make that mistake again, or I'll dock you for lost time."

"Only just a twisted German employee, I guess," thought Ned, as he was about to turn back. "I was mistaken. He probably didn't understand where he was sent."

He passed by the group of men, who, laughing and jeering at the German, were showing him where to go. He seemed to be a new hand in the works.

But as Ned passed he got one look at the man's face. Instead of a stupid countenance, for one instant he had a glimpse of the sharpest, brightest eyes he had ever looked into. And they were hard, cruel eyes, too, with a glint of daring in them. And, as Ned glanced at his figure, he thought he detected a trace of military stiffness—none of the stoop-shouldered slouch that is always the mark of a moulder. The fellow's hands, too, though black and grimy, showed evidences of care under the dirt, and Ned was sure his uncouth language was assumed.

"I'd like to know more about you," murmured Ned, but the man, with one sharp glance at him, passed on, seemingly to his own department of the works.

"Well, what was it?" asked Tom, as his chum rejoined him.

"Nothing very definite, but I'm sure there was something back of it all, Tom. I wouldn't be surprised but what that fellow—whoever he was—whatever his object was—hoped to get in to see the casting; either to get some idea about your new gun, or to do some desperate deed to spoil it."

"Do you think that, Ned?"

"I sure do. You've got to be on your guard, Tom."

"I will. But I wonder what object anyone could have in spoiling my gun?"

"So as to make his own cannon stand in a better light."

"Still thinking of General Waller, are you?"

"I am, Tom."

There was nothing more to be done at present, and, as it would take several days for the big mass of metal to properly cool, Tom, Ned and Mr. Damon returned to Shopton.

There Tom busied himself over many things. Ned helping him, and Mr. Damon lending an occasional hand. Koku was very useful, for often his great strength did what the combined efforts of Tom and his friends could not accomplish.

As for Eradicate, he "puttered around," doing all he could, which was not much, for he was getting old. Still Tom would not think of discharging him, and it was pitiful to see the old colored man try to do things for the young inventor—tasks that were beyond his strength. But if Koku offered to help, Eradicate would draw himself up, and exclaim:

"Git away fom heah! I guess dish yeah coon ain't forgot how t' wait on Massa Tom. Go 'way, giant. I ain't so big as yo'-all, but I know de English language, which is mo' 'n yo' all does. Go on an' lemme be!"

Koku, good naturedly, gave place, for he, too, felt for Eradicate.

"Well, Ned," remarked Tom one day, after the visit of the postman, "I have a letter from the steel people. They are going to take the gun out of the mould tomorrow, and start to rifle it. We'll take a run down in the airship, and see how it looks. I must take those drawings, too, that show the new plan of shrinking on the jackets. I guess I'll keep them in my room, so I won't forget them."

Tom and Ned occupied adjoining and connecting apartments, for, of late, Ned had taken up his residence with his chum. It was shortly after midnight that Ned was awakened by hearing someone prowling about his room. At first he thought it was Tom, for the shorter way to the bath lay through Ned's apartment, but when the lad caught the flash of a pocket electric torch he knew it could not be Tom.

"Who's there?" cried Ned sharply, sitting up in bed.

Instantly the light went out, and there was silence.

"Who's there?" cried Ned again.

This time he thought he heard a stealthy footstep.

"What is it?" called Tom from his chamber.

"Someone is in here!" exclaimed Ned. "Look out, Tom!"

CHAPTER XV

READY FOR THE TEST

Tom Swift acted promptly, for he realized the necessity. The events that had hedged him about since he had begun work on his giant cannon made him suspicious. He did not quite know whom to suspect, nor the reasons for their actions, but he had been on the alert for several days, and was now ready to act.

The instant Ned answered as he did, and warned Tom, the young inventor slid his hand under his pillow and pressed an auxiliary electric switch he had concealed there. In a moment the rooms were flooded with a bright light, and the two lads had a momentary glimpse of an intruder making a dive for the window.

"There he is, Tom!" cried Ned.

"What do you want?" demanded Tom, instinctively. But the intruder did not stay to answer.

Instead, he made a dive for the casement. It was one story above the ground, but this did not cause him any hesitation. It was summer, and the window was open, though a wire mosquito net barred the aperture. This was no hindrance to the man, however.

As Ned and Tom leaped from their beds, Ned catching up the heavy, empty water pitcher as a weapon, and Tom an old Indian war club that served as one of the ornaments of his room, the fellow, with one kick, burst the screen.

Then, clambering out on the sill, he dropped from sight, the boys hearing him land with a thud on the turf below. It was no great leap, though the fall must have jarred him considerably, for the boys heard him grunt, and then groan as if in pain.

"Quick!" cried Ned. "Ring the bell for Koku, Ned. I want to capture this fellow if possible."

"Who is he?" asked Ned.

"I don't know, but we'll see if we can size him up. Signal for the giant!"

There was an electric bell from Tom's room to the apartment of his big servant, and a speaking tube as well. While Ned was pressing the button, and hastily telling the giant what had happened, urging him to get in pursuit of the intruder, Tom had taken from his bureau a powerful, portable, electric flash lamp, of the same variety as that used by the would-be thief. Only Tom's was provided with a tungsten filament, which gave a glaring white pencil of light, increased by reflectors.

And in this glare the young inventor saw, speeding away over the lawn, the form of a big man.

"There he goes, Ned!" he shouted.

"So I see. Koku will be right on the job. I told him not to dress. Can you make out who the fellow is?"

"No, his back is toward us. But he's limping, all right. I guess that jump jarred him up a bit. Where is Koku?"

"There he goes now!" exclaimed Ned, as a figure leaped from the side door of the house—a gigantic figure, scantily clad.

"Get to him, Koku!" cried Tom.

"Me git, Master!" was the reply, and the giant sped on.

"Let's go out and lend a hand!" suggested Ned, looking at the water pitcher as though wondering what he had intended to do with it.

"I'm with you," agreed Tom. "Only I want to get into something a little more substantial than my pajamas."

As the two lads hurriedly slipped on some clothing they heard the voice of Mr. Swift calling:

"What is it, Tom? Has anything happened?"

"Nothing much," was the reassuring answer. "It was a near-happening, only Ned woke up in time. Someone was in our rooms—a burglar, I guess."

"A burglar! Good land a massy!" cried Eradicate, who had also gotten up to see what the excitement was about. "Did you cotch him, Massa Tom?"

"No, Rad; but Koku is after him."

"Koku? Huh, he nebber cotch anybody. I'se got t' git out dere mahse'f! Koku? Hu! I s'pects it's dat no-'count cousin ob mine, arter mah chickens ag'in! I'll lambaste dat coon when I gits him, so I will. I'll cotch him for yo'-all, Massa Tom," and, muttering to himself, the aged colored man endeavored to assume the activity of former years.

"Hark!" exclaimed Ned, as he and Tom were about ready to take part in the chase. "What's that noise, Tom?"

"Sounds like a motor-cycle."

"It is. That fellow—"

67

"It's the same chap!" interrupted Tom. "No use trying to chase him on that speedy machine. He's a mile away from here by now. He must have had it in waiting, ready for use. But come on, anyhow."

"Where are you going?"

"Out to the shop. I want to see if he got in there."

"But the charged wires?"

"He may have cut them. Come on."

It was as Tom had suspected. The deadly, charged wires, that formed a protecting cordon about his shops, had been cut, and that by an experienced hand, probably by someone wearing rubber gloves, who must have come prepared for that very purpose. During the night the current was supplied to the wires from a storage battery, through an intensifying coil, so that the charge was only a little less deadly than when coming direct from a dynamo.

"This looks bad, Tom," said Ned.

"It does, but wait until we get inside and look around. I'm glad I took my gun-plans to the house with me."

But a quick survey of the shop did not reveal any damage done, nor had anything been taken, as far as Tom could tell. The office of his main shop was pretty well upset, and it looked as though the intruder had made a search for something, and, not finding it, had entered the house.

"It was the gun-plans he was after, all right," decided Tom. "And I believe it was the same fellow who has been making trouble for me right along."

"You mean General Waller?"

"No, that German—the one who was at the machine shop."

"But who is he—what is his object?"

"I don't know who he is, but he evidently wants my plans. Probably he's a disappointed inventor, who has been trying to make a gun himself, and can't. He wants some of my ideas, but he isn't going to get them. Well, we may as well get back to bed, after I connect these wires again. I must think up a plan to conceal them, so they can't be cut."

While Tom and Ned were engaged on this, Koku came back, much out of breath, to report:

"Me not git, Master. He git on bang-bang machine and go off—puff!"

"So we heard, Koku. Never mind, we'll get him yet."

68

"Hu! Ef I had de fust chanst at him, I'd a cotched dat coon suah!" declared Eradicate, following the giant. "Koku he done git in mah way!" and he glared indignantly at the big man.

"That's all right, Rad," consoled Tom. "You did your best. Now we'll all get to bed. I don't believe he'll come back." Nor did he.

Tom and Ned were up at the first sign of daylight, for they wanted to go to the steel works, some miles away, in time to see the cannon taken out of the mould, and preparations made for boring the rifle channels. They found the manager, anxiously waiting for them.

"Some of my men are as interested in this as you are," he said to the young inventor. "A number of them declare that the cast will be a failure, while some think it will be a success."

"I think it will be all right, if my plans were followed," said Tom. "However, we'll see. By the way, what became of that German who made such a disturbance the day we cast the core?"

"Oh, you mean Baudermann?"

"Yes."

"Why, it's rather queer about him. The foreman of the shop where he was detailed, saw that he was an experienced man, in spite of his seemingly stupid ways, and he was going to promote him, only he never came back."

"Never came back? What do you mean?"

"I mean the day after the cast of the gun was made he disappeared, and never came back."

"Oh!" exclaimed Tom. He said nothing more, but he believed that he understood the man's actions. Failing to obtain the desired information, or perhaps failing to spoil the cast, he realized that his chances were at an end for the present.

With great care the gun was hoisted from the mould. More eyes than Tom's anxiously regarded it as it came up out of the casting pit.

"Bless my buttonhook!" cried Mr. Damon, who had gone with the lads. "It's a monster; isn't it?"

"Oh, wait until you see it with the jackets on!" exclaimed," Ned, who had viewed the completed drawings. "Then you'll open your eyes."

The great piece of hollow steel tubing was lifted to the boring lathe. Then Tom and the manager examined it for superficial flaws.

69

"Not one!" cried the manager in delight.

"Not that I can see," added Tom.. "It's a success—so far."

"And that was the hardest part of the work," went on the manager of the steel plant. "I can almost guarantee you success from now on."

And, as far as the rifling was concerned, this was true. I will not weary you with the details of how the great core of Tom Swift's giant cannon was bored. Sufficient to say that, after some annoying delays, caused by breaks in the machinery, which had never before been used on such a gigantic piece of work, the rifling was done. After the jackets had been shrunk on, it would be rifled again, to make it true in case of any shrinkage.

Then came the almost Herculean task of shrinking on the great red-hot steel jackets and wire-windings, that would add strength to the great cannon. To do this the central core was set up on end, and the jackets, having been heated in an immense furnace, were hoisted by a great crane over the core, and lowered on it as one would lower his napkin ring over the rolled up napkin.

It took weeks of hard work to do this, and Tom and Ned, with Mr. Damon occasionally for company, remained almost constantly at the plant. But finally the cannon was completed, the rifling was done over again to correct any imperfections, and the manager said:

"Your cannon is completed, Mr. Swift. I want to congratulate you on it. Never have we done such a stupendous piece of work. Only for your plans we could not have finished it. It was too big a problem for us. Your cannon is completed, but, of course, it will have to be mounted. What about the carriage?"

"I have plans for that," replied Tom; "but for the present I am going to put it on a temporary one. I want to test the gun now. It looks all right, but whether it will shoot accurately, and for a greater distance than any cannon has ever sent a projectile before, is yet to be seen."

"Where will you test it?"

"That is what we must decide. I don't want to take it too far from here. Perhaps you can select a place where it would be safe to fire it, say with a range of about thirty miles."

"Thirty miles! why, my dear sir—"

"Oh, I'm not altogether sure that it will go that distance," interrupted Tom, with a smile; "but I'm going to try for it, and I want to be on the safe side. Is there such a place near here?"

"Yes, I guess we can pick one out. I'll let you know."

"Then I must get back and arrange for my powder supply," went on the young inventor. "We'll soon test my giant cannon!"

"Bless my ear-drums!" cried Mr. Damon. "I hope nothing bursts. For if that goes up, Tom Swift—"

"I'm not making it to burst," put in Tom, with a smile. "Don't worry. Now, Ned, back to Shopton to get ready for the test."

CHAPTER XVI

A WARNING

"Whew, how it rains!" exclaimed Ned, as he looked out of the window.

"And it doesn't seem to show any signs of letting up," remarked Tom. "It's been at it nearly a week now, and it is likely to last a week longer."

"It's beastly," declared his chum. "How can you test your gun in this weather?"

"I can't. I've got to wait for it to clear."

"Bless my rubber boots! it's just got to stop some time," declared Mr. Damon. "Don't worry, Tom."

"But I don't like this delay. I have heard that General Waller has perfected a new gun—and it's a fine one, from all accounts. He has the proving grounds at Sandy Hook to test his on, and I'm handicapped here. He may beat me out."

"Oh, I hope not, Tom!" exclaimed Ned. "I'm going to see what the weather reports say," and he went to hunt up a paper.

It was several weeks after the completion of Tom's giant cannon. In the meanwhile the gun had been moved by the steel company to a little-inhabited part of New York State, some miles from the plant. The gun had been mounted on an improvised carriage, and now Tom and his friends were waiting anxiously for a chance to try it.

The work was not complete, for the steel company employees had been hampered by the rain. Never before, it seemed, had there been so much water coming down from the clouds. Nearly every day was misty, with gradations from mere drizzles to heavy downpours. There were occasional clear stretches, however, and during them the men worked.

A few more days of clear weather would be needed before the gun could be fastened securely to the carriage, and then Tom could fire one of the great projectiles that had been cast for it. Not until then would he know whether or not his cannon was going to be a success.

Meanwhile nothing more had been heard or seen of the spy. He appeared to have given up his attempts to steal Tom's secret, or to spoil his plans, if such was his object.

The place of the test, as I have said, was in a deserted spot. On one side of a great valley the gun was being set up. Its muzzle pointed up the valley, toward the side of a mountain, into which the gigantic projectile could plow its way without doing any damage. Tom was going to fire two kinds of cannon balls—a solid one, and one containing an explosive.

The gun was so mounted that the muzzle could be elevated or depressed, or swung from side to side. In this way the range could be varied. Tom estimated that the greatest possible range would be thirty miles. It could not be more than that, he decided, and he hoped it would not be much less. This extreme range could be attained by elevating the gun to exactly the proper pitch. Of course, any shorter range could, within certain limits, also be reached.

The gun was pointed slantingly up the valley, and there was ample room to attain the thirty-mile range without doing any damage.

At the head of the valley, some miles from where the giant cannon was mounted, was an immense dam, built recently by a water company for impounding a stream and furnishing a supply of drinking water for a distant city. At the other end of the valley was the thriving village of Preston. A railroad ran there, and it was to Preston station that Tom's big gun had been sent, to be transported afterward, on specially made trucks, drawn by powerful autos, to the place where it was now mounted.

Tom had been obliged to buy a piece of land on which to build the temporary carriage, and also contract for a large slice of the opposite mountain, as a target against which to fire his projectiles.

The valley, as I have said, was desolate. It was thickly wooded in spots, and in the centre, near the big dam, which held back the waters of an immense artificial lake, was a great hill, evidently a relic of some glacial epoch. This hill was a sort of division between two valleys.

Tom, Ned, Mr. Damon, with Koku, and some of the employees of the steel company, had hired a deserted farmhouse not far from the place where the gun was being mounted. In this they lived, while Tom directed operations.

"The paper says 'clear' tomorrow," read Ned, on his return. "'Clear, with freshening winds.'"

"That means rain, with no wind at all," declared Tom, with a sigh. "Well, it can't be helped. As Mr. Damon says, it will clear some time."

"Bless my overshoes!" exclaimed the odd gentleman. "It always has cleared; hasn't it?"

No one could deny this.

There came a slackening in the showers, and Tom and Ned, donning raincoats, went out to see how the work was progressing. They found the men from the steel concern busy at the great piece of engineering.

"How are you coming on?" asked Tom of the foreman.

"We could finish it in two days if this rain would only let up," replied the man.

"Well, let's hope that it will," observed Tom.

"If it doesn't, there's likely to be trouble up above," went on the foreman, nodding in the direction of the great dam.

"What do you mean?"

"I mean that the water is getting too high. The dam is weakening, I heard."

"Is that so? Why, I thought they had made it to stand any sort of a flood."

"They evidently didn't count on one like this. They've got the engineer who built it up there, and they're doing their best to strengthen it. I also heard that they're preparing to dynamite it to open breeches here and there in it, in case it is likely to give way suddenly."

"You don't mean it! Say, if it does go out with a rush it will wipe out the village."

"Yes, but it can't hurt us," went on the foreman. "We're too high up on the side of the hill. Even if the dam did burst, if the course of the water could be changed, to send it down that other valley, it would do no harm, for there are no settlements over there," and he pointed to the distant hill.

It was near this hill that Tom intended to direct his projectiles, and on the other side of it was another valley, running at right angles to the one crossed by the dam.

As the foreman had said, if the waters (in case the dam burst) could be turned into this transverse valley, the town could be saved.

"But it would take considerable digging to open a way through that side of the mountain, into the other valley," went on the man.

"Yes," said Tom, and then he gave the matter no further thought, for something came up that needed his attention.

"Have you your explosive here?" asked the foreman of the young inventor the next day, when the weather showed signs of clearing.

"Yes, some of it," said Tom. "I have another supply in a safe place in the village. I didn't want to bring too much here until the gun was to be fired. I can easily get it if we need it. Jove! I wish it would clear. I want to get out in my Humming Bird, but I can't if this keeps up." Tom had brought one of his speedy little airships with him to Preston.

The following day the clouds broke a little, and on the next the sun shone. Then the work on the gun went on apace. Tom and his friends were delighted.

"Well, I think we can try a shot tomorrow!" announced Tom with delight on the evening of the first clear day, when all hands had worked at double time.

"Bless my powder-horn!" exclaimed Mr. Damon. "You don't mean it!"

"Yes, the gun is all in place," went on the young inventor. "Of course, it's only a temporary carriage, and not the disappearing one I shall eventually use. But it will do. I'm going to try a shot tomorrow. Everything is in readiness."

There came a knock on the door of the room Tom had fitted up as an office in the old farmhouse.

"Who is it?" he asked.

"Me—Koku," was the answer.

"Well, what do you want, Koku?"

"Man here say him must see Master."

Tom and Ned looked at each other, suspicion in their eyes.

"Maybe it's that spy again," whispered Ned.

"If it is, we'll be ready for him," murmured his chum. "Show him in, Koku, and you come in too."

But the man who entered at once disarmed suspicion. He was evidently a workman from the dam above, and his manner was strangely excited.

"You folks had better get out of here!" he exclaimed.

"Why?" asked Tom, wondering what was going to happen.

"Why? Because our dam is going to burst within a few hours. I've been sent to warn the folks in town in time to let them take to the hills. You'd better move your outfit. The dam can't last twenty-four hours longer!"

CHAPTER XVII

THE BURSTING DAM

"Bless my fountain pen!" exclaimed Mr. Damon. "You don't mean it!"

"I sure do!" went on the man who had brought the startling news. "And the folks down below aren't going to have any more time than they need to get out of the way. They'll have to lose some of their goods, I reckon. But I thought I'd stop on my way down and warn you. You'd better be getting a hustle on."

"It's very kind of you," spoke Tom; "but I don't fancy we are in any danger."

"No danger!" cried the man. "Say, when that water begins to sweep-down here nothing on earth can stop it. That big gun of yours, heavy as it is, will be swept away like a straw, I know—I saw the Johnstown flood!"

"But we're so high up on the side of the hill, that the water won't come here," put in Ned. "We had that all figured out when we heard the dam was weak. We're not in any danger; do you think so, Tom?"

"Well, I hardly do, or I would not have set the gun where I did. Tell me," he went on to the man, "is there any way of opening the dam, to let the water out gradually?"

"There is, but the openings are not enough with such a flood as this. The engineers never counted on so much rain. It's beyond any they ever had here. You see, there was a small creek that we dammed up to make our lake. Some of the water from the spillway flows into that now, but its channel won't hold a hundredth part of the flood if the dam goes out.

"You'd better move, I tell you. The dam is slowly weakening. We've done all we can to save it, but that's out of the question. The only thing to do is to run while there's time. We've tried to make additional openings, but we daren't make any more, or the wall will be so weakened that it will go out in less than twenty-four hours.

"You've had your warning, now profit by it!" he added. "I'm going to tell those poor souls down in the valley below. It will be tough on them; but it can't be helped."

"If the dam bursts and the water could only be turned over into the transverse valley, this one would be safe," said Tom, in a low voice.

"Yes, but it can't be done!" the messenger exclaimed. "Our engineers thought of that, but it would take a week to open a channel, and there isn't time. It can't be done!"

"Maybe it can," spoke Tom, softly, but no one asked him what he meant.

"Well, I must be off," the man went on. "I've done my duty in warning you."

"Yes, you have," agreed Tom, "and if any damage comes to us it will be our own fault. But I don't believe there will."

The man hastened out, murmuring something about "rash and foolhardy people."

"What are you going to do, Tom?" asked Ned.

"Stay right here."

"But if the dam bursts?"

"It may not, but, if it does, we'll be safe. I have had a look at the water, and there's no chance for it to rise here, even if the whole dam went out at once, which is not likely. Don't worry. We'll be all right."

"Bless my checkbook!" cried Mr. Damon. "But what about those poor people in the valley?"

"They will have time to flee, and save their lives," spoke the young inventor; "but they may lose their homes. They can sue the water company for damages, though. Now don't do any more worrying, but get to bed, and be ready for the test tomorrow. And the first thing I do I'm going to have a little flight in the Humming Bird to get my nerves in trim. This long rain has gotten me in poor shape. Koku, you must be on the alert tonight. I don't want anything to happen to my gun at the last minute."

"Me watch!" exclaimed the giant, significantly, as he picked up a heavy club.

"Do you anticipate any trouble?" asked Ned, anxiously.

"No, but it's best to be on the safe side," answered Tom. "Now let's turn in."

Certainly the next day, bright and sunshiny as it broke, had in it little of impending disaster. The weather was fine after the long-continued rains, and the whole valley seemed peaceful and quiet. At the far end could be seen the great dam, with water pouring over it in a thin sheet, forming a small stream that trickled down the centre of the valley, and to the town below.

But, through great pipes that led to the drinking system, though they were unseen, thundered immense streams of solid water, reducing by as much as the engineers were able the pressure on the concrete wall.

Tom and Ned, in the Humming Bird, took a flight out to the dam shortly after breakfast, when the steel men were putting a few finishing touches to the gun carriage, ready for the test that was to take place about noon.

"It doesn't look as though it would burst," observed Ned, as the aircraft hovered over the big artificial lake.

"No," agreed Tom. "But I suppose the engineers want to be on the safe side in case of damage suits. I want to take a look at the place where the other valley comes up to this at right angles."

He steered his powerful little craft in that direction, and circled low over the spot.

"A bursting projectile, about where that big white stone is, would do the trick," murmured Tom.

"What trick?" asked Ned, curiously.

"Oh, I guess I was talking to myself," admitted Tom, with a laugh. "I may not have to do it, Ned."

"Well, you're talking in riddles today, all right, Tom. When you get ready to put me wise, please do."

"I will. Now we'll get back, and fire our first long shot. I do hope I make a record."

There was much to be done, in spite of the fact that the foreman of the steel workers assured Tom that all was in readiness. It was some time that afternoon when word was given for those who wished to retire to an improvised bomb-proof. Word had previously been sent down the valley so that no one, unless he was looking for trouble, need be in the vicinity of the gun, nor near where the shots were to land.

Through powerful glasses Tom and Ned surveyed the distant mountain that was to be the target. Several great squares of white cloth had been put at different bare spots to make the finding of the range easy.

"I guess we're ready now," announced the young inventor, a bit nervously. "Bring up the powder, Koku."

"Me bring," exclaimed the giant, calmly, as he went to the bomb-proof where the powerful explosive was kept.

The great projectile was in readiness to be slung into the breech by means of the hoisting apparatus, for it weighed close to two tons. It was carefully inserted under Tom's supervision. It carried no bursting charge, for Tom's first shot was merely to establish the extreme range that his cannon would shoot.

"Now the powder," called the young inventor. To avoid accidents Koku handled this himself, the hoisting apparatus being dispensed with. Tom figured out that five hundred pounds of his new, powerful explosive would be about the right amount to use, and this quantity, divided into several packages to make the handling easier, was quickly inserted in the breech of the gun by Koku.

"Bless my doormat!" cried Mr. Damon, who stood near, looking nervously on. "Don't drop any of that."

"Me no drop," was the answer.

Tom was busily engaged in figuring on a bit of paper, and Ned, who looked over his shoulder, saw a complicated compilation that looked to be a combination of geometry, algebra, differential calculus and other higher mathematics.

"What are you doing, Tom?" he asked.

"I'm trying to confirm my own theories by means of figures, to see if I can really reach that farthest target."

"What, not the one thirty miles away.

"That's it, Ned. I want to get a thirty-mile range if I can."

"It isn't possible, Tom."

"Bless my tape measure! I should say not!" cried Mr. Damon.

"We'll see," replied Tom, quietly. "Put in the primer, Ned; and, Koku, close the breech and slot it home."

In a few seconds the great gun was ready for firing.

"Now," said Tom, "this thing may be all right, and it may not. The only thing that can cause an accident will be a flaw in the steel. No one can guard against that. So, in order to be on the safe side, we will all go into the bomb-proof, and I will fire the gun from there. The wires are long enough."

They all agreed that this was good advice, and soon the steel men and Tom's friends were gathered in a sort of cave that had been hollowed out in the side of the hill, and at an angle from the big gun.

"If it does burst—which I hope it won't," said Tom, "the pieces will fly in straight lines, so we will be safe enough here. Ned, are you are ready at the instruments?"

"Yes, Tom."

"I want you to note the registered muzzle velocity. Mr. Damon, you will please read the pressure gauge. After I press the button I'm going to watch the landing of the projectile through the telescope."

The gun had been pointed, as I have said, at the farthest target—one thirty miles away, telescope sights on the giant cannon making this possible.

"All ready!" cried Tom.

"All ready," answered Ned.

There was a tense moment; Tom's thumb pressed home the electric button, and then came the explosion.

It seemed for a moment as if everyone was lifted from his feet. They had all stood on their tiptoes, and opened their mouths to lessen the shock, but even then it was terrific. The very ground shook—from the roof of their cave small stones and gravel rattled down on their heads. Their ear-drums were numbed from the shock. And the noise that filled the valley seemed like a thousand thunderbolts merged into one.

Tom rushed from the bombproof, dropping the electric button. He caught sight of his gun, resting undisturbed on the improvised carriage.

"Hurray!" he cried in delight. "She stood the charge all right. And look! look!" he cried, as he pointed the glasses toward the distant hillside. "There goes my projectile as straight as an arrow. There! By Caesar, Ned! It landed within three feet of the target! Oh, you beauty!" he yelled at his giant cannon. "You did all I hoped you would! Thirty miles, Ned! Think of that! A two-ton projectile being shot thirty miles!"

"It's great, Tom!" yelled his chum, clapping him on the back, and capering about. "It's the longest shot on record."

"It certainly is," declared the foreman of the steel workers, who had helped in casting many big guns. "No cannon ever made can equal it. You win, Tom Swift!"

"Bless my armor plate!" gasped Mr. Damon. "What attacking ship against the Panama Canal could float after a shot like that."

"Not one," declared Tom; "especially after I put a bursting charge into the projectile. We'll try that next."

By means of compressed air the gases and some particles of the unexploded powder were blown out of the big cannon. Then it was loaded again, the projectile this time carrying a bursting charge of another explosive that would be set off by concussion.

Once more they retired to the bombproof, and again the great gun was fired. Once more the ground shook, and they were nearly deafened by the shock.

Then, as they looked toward the distant hillside, they saw a shower of earth and great rocks rise up. It was like a sand geyser. Then, when this settled back again, there was left a gaping hole in the side of the mountain.

"That does the business!" cried Tom. "My cannon is a success!"

The last shot did not go quite as far as the first, but it was because a different kind of projectile was used. Tom was perfectly satisfied, however. Several more trials were given the gun, and each one confirmed the young inventor in his belief that he had made a wonderful weapon.

"If that doesn't fortify the Panama Canal nothing will," declared Ned.

"Well, I hope I can convince Uncle Sam of that," spoke Tom, simply.

The muzzle velocity and the pressure were equal to Tom's highest hopes. He knew, now, that he had hit on just the right mixture of powder, and that his gun was correctly proportioned. It showed not the slightest strain.

"Now we'll try another bursting shell," he said, after a rest, during which some records were made. "Then we'll call it a day's work. Koku, bring up some more powder. I'll use a little heavier charge this time."

It was while the gun was being loaded that a horseman was seen riding wildly down the valley. He was waving a red flag in his hand.

"Bless my watch chain!" cried Mr. Damon. "What's that?"

"It looks as though he was coming to give us a warning," suggested the steel foreman.

"Maybe someone has kicked about our shooting," remarked Ned.

"I hope not," murmured Tom.

He looked at the horseman anxiously. The rider came nearer and nearer, wildly waving his flag. He seemed to be shouting something, but his words could not be made out. Finally he came near enough to be heard.

"The dam! The dam!" he cried. "It's bursting. Your shots have hastened it. The cracks are widening. You'd better get away!" And he galloped on.

"Bless my toilet soap!" gasped Mr. Damon.

"I was afraid of this!" murmured Tom. "But, since our shots have hastened the disaster, maybe we can avert it."

"How?" demanded Ned.

"I'll show you. All hands come here and we'll shift this gun. I want it to point at that big white stone!" and he indicated an immense boulder, well up the valley, near the place where the two great gulches joined.

CHAPTER XVIII

THE DOPED POWDER

"What are you going to do, Tom?" cried Ned, as he, with the others, worked the hand gear that shifted the big gun. When it was permanently mounted electricity would accomplish this work. "What's your game, Tom?"

"Don't you remember, Ned? When we were talking about the chance of the dam bursting, I said if the current of suddenly released water could be turned into the other valley, the people below us would be saved."

"Yes."

"Well, that's what I'm going to do. I'm going to fire a bursting shell at the point where the two valleys come together. I'll break down the barrier of rock and stone between them."

"Bless my shovel and hoe!" cried Mr. Damon.

"If we can turn enough of the water into the other valley, where no one lives, and where it can escape into the big river there, the amount that will flow down this valley will be so small that only a little damage will be done."

"That's right!" declared the steel foreman, as he caught Tom's idea. "It's the only way it could be done, too, for there won't be time to make the necessary excavation any other way. Is the gun swung around far enough, Mr. Swift?"

"No, a little more toward me," answered Tom, as he peered through the telescope sights. "There, that will do. Now to get the proper elevation," and he began to work the other apparatus, having estimated the range as well as he could.

In a few seconds the giant cannon was properly trained on the white rock. Meanwhile the horseman, with his red flag, had continued on down the valley. In spite of his warning of the night before, it developed that a number had disregarded it, and had remained in their homes. Most of the inhabitants, however, had fled to the hills, to stay in tents, or with such neighbors as could accommodate them. Some lingered to move their household goods, while others fled with what they could carry.

It was to see that the town was deserted by these late-stayers that the messenger rode, crying his warning as did the messenger at the bursting of the Johnstown dam twenty-odd years ago.

"The projectile!" cried Tom, as he saw that all was in readiness. "Lively now! I can see the top of the dam beginning to crumble," and he laid aside the telescope he had been using.

The projectile, with a heavy charge of bursting powder, was slung into the breech of the gun.

"Now the powder, Koku!" called Tom. "Be quick; but not so fast that you drop any of it."

"Me fetch," responded the giant, as he hastened toward the small cave where the explosive was kept. As the big man brought the first lot, and Ned was about to insert it in the breech of the gun, behind the projectile, Tom exclaimed:

"Just let me have a look at that. It's some that I first made, and I want to be sure it hasn't gone stale."

Critically he looked at the powerful explosive. As he did so a change came over his face.

"Here, Koku!" the young inventor said. "Where did you get this?"

"In cave, Master."

"Is there any more left?"

"Only enough for this one shoot."

"By Jove!" muttered Tom. "There's been some trick played here!" and he set off on a run toward the bomb-proof.

"What's the matter?" cried Ned, as he noticed the agitation of his chum.

"The powder has been doped!" yelled Tom. "Something has been put in it to make it nonexplosive. It's no good. It wouldn't send that shell a thousand yards, and it's got to go five miles to do any good. My plan won't work."

"Doped the powder?" gasped Ned. "Who could have done it?"

"I don't know. There must have been some spy at work. Quick, run and ask the foreman if any of his men are missing. I'll see if there's enough of the good powder left to break down the barrier!"

Ned was away like a shot, while the others, not knowing what to make of the strange conduct of the two lads, looked on in wonder. Tom raced toward the cave where the powder was stored, Koku following him.

"Bless my shoe laces!" cried Mr. Damon. "Look at the dam now!"

They gazed to where he pointed. In several places the concrete spillway had crumbled down to a ragged edge, showing that the solid wall was giving way. The amount of water flowing over the dam was greater now. The creek was steadily rising. Down the valley the horseman with the red flag was but a speck in the distance.

"What can I do? What can I do?" murmured Tom. "If all the powder there is left has been doped, I can't save the town! What can I do? What can I do?"

Ned had reached the foreman, who, with his helpers, was standing about the big gun.

"Have any of your men left recently?" yelled Ned.

"Any of my men left? What do you mean?

"Schlichter went yesterday," said the timekeeper. "I thought he was in quite a hurry to get his money, too."

"Schlichter gone!" exclaimed the foreman. "He was no good anyhow. I think he was a sort of Anarchist; always against the government, the way he talked. So he has left; eh? But what's the matter, Ned?"

"Something wrong with the powder. Tom can't shoot the cannon and turn aside the water to save the town. Some of his enemies have been at work. Schlichter leaving at this time, and in such hurry, makes it look suspicious."

"It sure does! And, now I recall it, I saw him yesterday near your powder magazine. I called him down for it, for I knew Tom Swift had given orders that only his own party was to go near it. So the powder is doped; eh?"

"Yes! It's all off now."

He turned to see Tom approaching on the run.

"Any good powder left?" asked Ned.

"Not a pound. Did you hear anything?"

"Yes, one man has disappeared. Oh, Tom, we've got to fail after all! We can't save the town!"

"Yes, we can, Ned. If that dam will only hold for half an hour more."

"What do you mean

"I mean that I have another supply of good powder in the village. I secreted some there, you remember I told you. If I can go get that, and get back here in time, I can break down the barrier with one shot, and save Preston."

"But you never can make the trip there and back in time, with the powder, Tom. It's impossible. The dam may hold half an hour, or it may not. But, if it does, you can't do anything!"

"I can't? Well, I'm going to make a big try, Ned. You stay on the job here. Have everything ready so that when I get back with the new explosive, which

I hope hasn't been tampered with, I can shove it into the breech, and set it off. Have the wires, primers and button all ready for me."

Then Tom set off on the run.

"Where are you going?" gasped his chum. "You can never run to Preston and back in time."

"I don't intend to. I'm going in my airship. Koku, never mind bringing the rest of the powder from the cave. It's no good. Run out the Humming Bird. I'm going to drive her to the limit. I've just got to get that powder here on time!"

"Bless my timetable!" gasped Mr. Damon. "That's the only way it can be done. Lucky Tom brought the airship along!"

The young inventor, pausing only to get some cans for the explosive, and some straps with which to fasten them in the monoplane, leaped into the speedy craft.

The motor was adjusted; Koku whirled the propeller blades. There was a staccato succession of explosions, a rushing, roaring sound, and then the craft rose like a bird, and Tom circled about, making a straight course for the distant town, while below him the creek rose higher and higher as the dam continued to crumble away.

CHAPTER XIX

BLOWING DOWN THE BARRIER

"Can you see anything of him, Ned?"

"Not a thing, Mr. Damon. Wait—hold on—no! It's only a bird," and the lad lowered the glasses with which he had been sweeping the sky. looking for his chum returning in his airship with the powder.

"He'd better hurry," murmured the foreman. "That dam can't last much longer. The water is rising fast. When it does go out it will go with a rush. Then good-bye to the village of Preston."

"Bless my insurance policy!" cried Mr. Damon. "Don't say such things, my friend."

"But they're true!" insisted the man. "You can see for yourself that the cracks in the dam are getting larger. It will be a big flood when it does come. And I'm not altogether sure that we're safe up here," he added, as he looked down the sides of the hill to where the creek was now rapidly becoming a raging torrent.

"Bless my hat-band!" gasped Mr. Damon. "You—you are getting on my nerves!"

"I don't want to be a calamity howler," went on the foreman; "but we've got to face this thing. We'd better get ready to vamoose if Tom Swift doesn't reach here in time to fire that shot—and he doesn't seem to be in sight."

Once more Ned swept the sky with his glasses. The roar of the water below them could be plainly heard now.

"I wish I could get hold of that rascally German," muttered the foreman. "I'd give him more than a piece of my mind. It will be his fault if the town is destroyed, for Tom's plan would have saved it. I wonder who he can be, anyhow?"

"Some spy," declared Ned. "We've been having trouble right along, you know, and this is part of the game. I have some suspicions, but Tom doesn't agree with me. Certainly the fellow, whatever his object, has made trouble enough this time."

"I should say so," agreed the foreman.

"Look, Ned!" cried Mr. Damon. "Is that a bird; or is it Tom?" and he pointed to a speck in the sky. Ned quickly focused his glasses on it.

"It's Tom!" he cried a second later. "It's Tom in the Humming Bird!"

"Thank Heaven for that!" exclaimed Mr. Damon, fervently, forgetting to bless anything on this occasion. "If only he can get here in time!"

"He's driving her to the limit!" cried Ned, still watching his chum through the glass. "He's coming!"

"He'll need to," murmured the foreman, grimly. "That dam can't last ten minutes more. Look at the people fleeing from the valley!"

He pointed to the north, and a confused mass of small black objects—men, women and children, doubtless, who had lingered in spite of the other warning—could be seen clambering up the sides of the valley.

"Is everything ready at the gun?" asked Mr. Damon.

"Everything," answered Ned, whom Tom had instructed in all the essentials. "As soon as he lands we'll jam in the powder, and fire the shot."

"I hope he doesn't land too hard, with all that explosive on board," murmured the foreman.

"Bless my checkerboard!" cried Mr. Damon. "Don't suggest such a thing."

"I guess we can trust Tom," spoke Ned.

They looked up. The distant throb of the monoplane's motor could now be heard above the roar of the swollen waters. Tom could be seen in his seat, and beside him, in the other, was a large package.

Nearer and nearer came the monoplane. It began to descend, very gently, for well Tom Swift knew the danger of hitting the ground too hard with the cargo he carried.

He described a circle in the air to check his speed. Then, gently as a bird, he made a landing not far from the gun, the craft running easily over one of the few level places on the side of the hill. Tom yanked on the brake, and the iron-shod pieces of wood dug into the ground, checking the progress of the monoplane on its bicycle wheels.

"Have you got it, Tom?" yelled Ned.

"I have," was the answer of the young inventor as he leaped from his seat.

"Is it good powder?" asked the foreman, anxiously.

"I don't know," spoke Tom. "I didn't have time to look. I just rushed up to where I had stored it, got some out and came back with the motor at full speed. Ran into an airpocket, too, and I thought it was all up with me when I began to fall. But I managed to get out of it. Say, we're going to have it nip and tuck here to save the village."

"That's what!" agreed the foreman, as he helped Koku take the cans of explosive.

"Wait until I look at it," suggested Tom, as he opened one. His trained eye and touch soon told him that this explosive had not been tampered with.

"It's all right!" he shouted. "Into the gun with it, and we'll see what happens."

It was the work of only a few moments to put in the charge. Then, once more, the breech-block was slotted home, and the trailing electric wires unreeled to lead to the bomb-proof.

Tom Swift took one last look through the telescope sights of his giant cannon. He changed the range slightly by means of the hand and worm-screw gear, and then, with the others, ran to the shelter of the cave. For, though the gun had stood the previous tests well, Tom had used a heavier charge this time, both in the firing chamber and in the projectile, and he wanted to take no chances.

"All ready?" asked the young inventor, as he looked around at his friends gathered in the cave.

"I—I guess so," answered Ned, somewhat doubtfully.

Tom hesitated a moment, then, as his fingers stiffened to press the electric button there sounded to the ears of all a dull, booming sound.

"The dam! It has given way!" cried Ned.

"That's it!" shouted the foreman. "Fire!"

Tom pressed the button. Once again was that awful tremor of the earth—the racking shake—the terrific explosion and a shock that knocked a couple of the men down.

"All right!" shouted Tom. "The gun held together. It's safe to go out. We'll see what happened!"

They all rushed from the shelter of the cave. Before them was an awe-inspiring sight. A great wall of water was coming down the valley, from a large opening in the centre of the dam. It seemed to leap forward like a race horse.

Tom declared afterward that he saw his projectile strike the barrier that separated one valley from the other, but none of the others had eyesight as keen as this—and perhaps Tom was in error.

But there was no doubt that they all saw what followed. They heard a distant report as the great projectile burst. Then a wall of earth seemed to rise up in front of the advancing wall of water. High into the air great stones and masses of dirt were thrown.

"A good shot!" cried the foreman. "Just in the right place, Tom Swift!"

For a moment it was as though that wall of water hesitated, not deciding whether to continue on down the populated valley, or to swing over into the other gash where it could do comparatively little harm. It was a moment of suspense.

Then, as Tom's great shot had, by means of the exploding projectile, torn down the barrier, the water chose the more direct and shorter path. With a mighty roar, like a distant Niagara, it swept into the new channel the young inventor had made. Into the transverse valley it tumbled and tossed in muddy billows of foam, and only a small portion of the flood added itself to the already swollen creek.

The village of Preston had been saved by the shot from Tom's giant cannon.

CHAPTER XX

THE GOVERNMENT ACCEPTS

"Whew! Let me sit down somewhere and get my breath!" gasped Tom, when it was all over.

"I should think you would want a bit of quiet," replied Ned. "You've been on the jump since early morning."

"Bless my dining-room table!" cried Mr. Damon. "I should say so! I'll go tell the cook to get us all a good meal—we need it," for a competent cook had been installed in the old farmhouse where Tom and his party had their headquarters.

"But you did the trick, Tom, old man!" exclaimed Ned, fervently, as he looked down the valley and saw the receding water. For, with the opening of the channel into the other valley the flood, at no time particularly dangerous near Preston, was subsiding rapidly.

"He sure did," declared the foreman. "No one else could have done it, either."

"Oh, I don't know," spoke Tom, modestly. "It just happened so. There was one minute, though, after I got to the place in Preston where I had stored the powder, that I didn't know whether I would succeed or not."

"How was that?" asked Mr. Damon.

"Why, in my hurry and excitement I forgot the key to the underground storeroom where I had put the explosive. I knew there was no time to get another, so I took a chance and burst in the door with an axe I found in the freight depot."

"I should say you did take a chance!" declared Ned, who knew how "freaky" the high explosive was, and how likely it was, at times, to be set off by the least concussion.

"But it came out all right," went on Tom. "I bundled it into the other seat of my Humming Bird, and started back."

"Had most of the folks left town?" asked the foreman.

"Nearly all," replied Tom. "The last of them were hurrying away as I left. And it shows how scared they were, they didn't pay any attention to me and my flying machine, though I'll wager some of them never saw one before."

"Well, they don't need to be scared any more," put in Mr. Damon "You saved their homes for them, Tom."

"I'd like to get hold of the fellow who doped my powder; that's what I'd like to do," murmured the young inventor. "Ned, we'll have to be doubly watchful from now on. But I must take a look at my gun. That last charge may have strained it."

But the giant cannon was as perfect as the day it was turned out of the shop. Not even the extra charge of the powerful explosive had injured it.

"That's fine!" cried Tom, as he looked at every part. "As soon as this flood is over we'll try some more practice shots. But we're all entitled to a rest now."

The great gun was covered with tarpaulins to protect it from the weather, and then all retired to the house for a bountiful meal. Late that afternoon nearly all signs of the flood had disappeared, save that along the edges of the creek was much driftwood, showing the height to which the creek had risen. But it would have gone much higher had it not been for Tom's timely shot.

The water from the impounded lake continued to pour down into the cross valley, and did some damage, but nothing like what would have followed its advent into Preston. The few inhabitants of the gulch into which the young inventor had directed the flood had had warning, and had fled in time. In Preston, some few houses nearest the banks of the rising creek were flooded, but were not carried away.

The following day some of the officers of the water company paid a visit to Tom, to thank him for what he had done. But for him they would have been responsible for great property damage, and loss of life might have followed.

They intended to rebuild the dam, they said, on a new principle, making it much stronger.

"And," said the president, "we will have an emergency outlet gate into that valley you so providentially opened for us, Mr. Swift. Then, in time of great rain, we can let the water out slowly as we need to."

Tom's chief anxiety, now, was to bring his perfected gun to the notice of the United States Government officials. To have them accept it, he knew he must give it a test before the ordnance board, and before the officers of the army and navy. Accordingly he prepared for this.

He ordered several new projectiles, some of a different type from those heretofore used, and leaving Koku and Ned in charge of the gun, went back to Shopton to superintend the manufacture of an additional supply of his explosive. He took care, too, that no spies gained access to it.

Then, with a plentiful supply of ammunition and projectiles, Tom resumed his practice in the lonely valley. He had, in the meanwhile, sent requests to the proper government officials to come and witness the tests.

At first he met with no success, and he learned, incidentally, that General Waller had built a new gun, the merits of which he was also anxious to show.

"It's a sort of rivalry between us," said Tom to Ned.

But, in a way, fortune favored our hero. For when General Waller tested his new gun, though it did not burst, it did not come up to expectations, and its range was not as great as some of the weapons already in use.

Then, too, Captain Badger acted as Tom's friend at court. He "pulled wires" to good advantage, and at last the government sent word that one of the ordnance officers would be present on a certain day to witness the tests.

"I wish the whole board had come," said Tom. "Probably they have only sent a young fellow, just out of West Point, who will turn me down.

"But I'm going to give him the surprise of his life; and if he doesn't report favorably, and insist on the whole board coming out here, I'll be much disappointed."

Tom made his preparations carefully, and certainly Captain Waydell, the young officer who came to represent Uncle Sam, was impressed. Tom sent shell after shell, heavily charged, against the side of the mountain. Great holes and gashes were torn in the earth. The gun even exceeded the range of thirty miles. And the heaviest armor plate that could be procured was to the projectiles of the giant cannon like cheese to a revolver bullet.

"It's great, Mr. Swift! Great!" declared the young captain. "I shall strongly recommend that the entire board see this test." And when Tom let him fire the gun himself the young man was more than delighted.

He was as good as his word, and a week later the entire ordnance board, from the youngest member to the grave and grizzled veterans, were present to witness the test of Tom's giant cannon.

It is needless to say that it was successful. Tom and Ned, not to mention Mr. Damon, Koku and every loyal member of the steel working gang, saw to it that there was no hitch. The solid shots were regarded with wonder, and when the explosive one was sent against the hillside, making a geyser of earth, the enthusiasm was unbounded.

"We shall certainly recommend your gun, Mr. Swift," declared the Chief of Staff. "It does just what we want it to do, and we have no doubt that

Congress will appropriate the money for several with which to fortify the Panama Canal."

"The gun is most wonderful," spoke a voice with a German accent. "It is surprising!"

Tom and Ned both started. They saw an officer, evidently a foreigner, resplendent in gold trimmings, and with many medals, standing near the secretary of the ordnance board.

"Yes, General von Brunderger," agreed the chief, "it is a most timely invention. Mr. Swift, allow me to present you to General von Brunderger, of the German army, who is here learning how Uncle Sam does things."

Tom bowed and shook hands. He glanced sharply at the German, but was sure he had never seen him before. Then all the board, and General von Brunderger, who, it appeared, was present as an invited guest, examined the big cannon critically, while Tom explained the various details.

When the board members left, the chief promised to let Tom know the result of the formal report as soon as possible.

The young inventor did not have long to wait. In about two weeks, during which time he and Ned perfected several little matters about the cannon, there came an official-looking document.

"Well, we'll soon know the verdict," spoke Tom, somewhat nervously, as he opened the envelope. Quickly he read the enclosure.

"What is it!" cried Ned.

"The government accepts my gun!" exclaimed the young inventor. "It will purchase a number as soon as they can be made. We are to take one to Panama, where it will be set up. Hurray, Ned, my boy! Now for Panama!"

CHAPTER XXI

OFF FOR PANAMA

"Well, Tom, it doesn't seem possible; does it, old man?"

"You're right, Ned—in a way. And yet, after all the hard work we've done, almost anything is possible."

"Hard work! We? Oh, pshaw! You've done most of it, Tom. I only helped here and there."

"Indeed, and you did more than that. If it hadn't been for you, Mr. Damon and Koku we'd never have gotten off as soon as we did. The government is the limit for doing things, sometimes."

"Bless my timetable! but I agree with you," put in Mr. Damon. "But at last we are on the way, in spite of delays."

This conversation took place on board one of Uncle Sam's warships, which the President had designated to take Tom's giant cannon to the Panama Canal.

The big gun had been lashed to the deck of the vessel, and was well protected from the weather. In the hold the parts of the disappearing carriage, which Tom had at last succeeded in having made, were securely stowed. In another part of the warship were the big projectiles, some arranged to be fired as solid shots, and others with a bursting charge. There was also a good supply of the powerful explosive, and Tom had taken extraordinary precautions so that it could not be tampered with. Koku had been detailed as a sort of guard over it, and to relieve him was a trustworthy sergeant of marines.

"If anyone tries to dope that powder now, and spoil my test at Panama," declared Tom, "he'll wish he'd never tried it."

"Especially if Koku gets hold of him," added Ned, grimly.

"But I don't believe there is any danger," went on the young inventor. "I spoke about what had happened, and the ordnance board took extra precautions to see that none but men and officers who could be implicitly trusted had anything to do with this expedition."

"You don't really believe anything like treachery would be attempted; do you, Tom?"

"I don't know what to say. Certainly I can't see why anyone connected with Uncle Sam would want to throw cold water on a plan to fortify the canal, even if an outsider has invented the gun—I mean someone like myself, not connected with the army or navy."

"If it's anything it's jealousy," declared Ned, "That General Waller—"

"There you go again, Ned. Let's not talk about it. Come on forward and see what progress we are making."

It must not be supposed that to get the big gun aboard the vessel, arrange for a new supply of the explosive, and for many of the great projectiles, had been easy work. It was a task that taxed the skill and strength of Tom and his friends to the utmost.

There had been wearying delays, especially in the matter of making the disappearing carriage. At times it seemed as if the required projectiles would never be finished. The powder, too, gave trouble, for sometimes batches would be turned out that were utterly worthless.

But Tom never gave up, even when it seemed that some of the failures were purposely made. Ned declared that there was a conspiracy against his chum, but Tom could not see it that way. It was due to a combination of circumstances, he insisted.

But finally the gun had been put aboard the ship, having been transported from the proving ground in the valley, and they were now en route to Panama. There the giant cannon was to be set up, and tried again. If it came up to expectations it was to be finally adopted as the official gun for the protection of the big canal, and Tom would receive a substantial reward.

"And I'm confident that it will make good," said the young inventor to his chum, as they paced the deck of the vessel. "In fact, I'm so sure I have practically engaged the Universal Steel Company to hold itself in readiness to make several more of the guns."

"But suppose Uncle Sam decides against the cannon on this second test?"

"Well, then I've lost out, that's all," declared Tom, philosophically. "But I don't believe they will."

"It certainly is a giant cannon," remarked Ned, as he paused to look at the prostrate monster, lashed to the deck, with its wrappings of tarpaulins. "It looks bigger here than it did when you fired the shot that saved the town, Tom."

"Yes, I suppose it does, by contrast. But let's go down and see how the powder and shells are standing the trip. I told the captain to have them securely lashed, so if we struck rough weather, and the vessel rolled, they wouldn't carry away."

"Especially the powder," put in Ned. "If that starts to banging around—well, I'd rather be somewhere else."

"Bless my rain gauge!" cried Mr. Damon. "Please don't say such things. You make me nervous. You're as bad as that steel foreman."

"All right, I'll be better," promised Ned, with a laugh.

The two chums found that every precaution had been taken in regard to the projectiles and powder. Koku was on guard, the giant regarding the boxes of explosive with a calm but determined eye. It would not be well for any unauthorized hand to tamper with them.

"Am dere anyt'ing I kin do fo' yo'-all, Massa Tom?" inquired Eradicate, as the young inventor and Ned prepared to go on deck again. The aged colored man had insisted on coming as a sort of personal bodyguard to Tom, and the latter had not the heart to refuse him. Eradicate was desperately jealous of the giant.

"Huh!" Eradicate had said, "anybody kin sit an' look at a lot ob dem powder boxes; but 'tain't everybody what kin wait on Massa Tom. I kin, an' I'se gwine t' do it." And so he had.

It was planned to proceed directly to Colon, the eastern terminus of the canal, from New York, stopping at Santiago to transact some government business there. The big gun was to be mounted on a barbette near the Gatun locks, pointing out to sea, and the trial shots would be fired over the water.

Eventually the gun would be so mounted as to swing in a circle, so as to command the land as well as the water; and, in fact, if the government decided to adopt Tom's giant cannon as the official protective arm of the canal, they would all be so mounted. For, of course, it might be possible for land as well as sea forces to attack and try to capture the big ditch.

The first few days of the voyage were pleasant enough. The weather was fine, and Tom was kept busy explaining to many of the officers aboard the ship the principles of his gun, powder and projectiles. Members of the ordnance board, who had been detailed to witness the test, were also much interested as Tom modestly described his work on the giant cannon.

At Santiago de Cuba, when Tom and Ned were standing near the gangway, watching the officers returning from shore leave, for the ship was to proceed soon, after a two days' stay, the young inventor started as he noticed a military man walking aboard.

"Look, Ned!" he exclaimed, in a low voice.

"Where?"

"At that man—an officer in civilian dress, I should judge—haven't you seen him before?"

"I have, Tom. Now, where was it? I seem to remember his face; and yet he wasn't dressed like this the last time I saw him."

"I guess not, Ned. He had on a uniform then."

"By jinks! I have it. That German officer—von Brunderger! That's he!"

"You're right, Ned. And he's got his servant with him, I guess," and Tom nodded toward a stolid German who was carrying the other's suitcase.

"I wonder what he's doing aboard here?" went on our hero's chum.

"We'll soon know," spoke Tom. "He's seen us and is nodding. We might as well go meet him."

"Ah, my good friend, Tom Swift!" exclaimed General von Brunderger, genially, as he grasped the hands of Tom and Ned. "I am glad to see you both again." He seemed to mean it, though he had not been especially cordial to them at the first gun test. "Take my grip below," he said in German to the man, "and, Rudolph, find Lieutenant Blake and inform him that I am on board. I have been invited to go to Panama by Lieutenant Blake," he added to Tom. "I have never seen the big ditch that you wonderful Americans have so nearly finished."

"It is going to be a big thing," spoke Tom. "I am proud that my gun is going to help protect it."

"Ah, so you were successful, then?" and his voice expressed surprise. "I had not heard. And the big gun; is he here?" Though speaking very good English, von Brunderger occasionally lapsed into the idioms of his Fatherland.

"Yes, it's on board," said Tom. "Are you going to Panama for any special purpose?"

Ned declared afterward that the German started as Tom asked this question, but if he did the young inventor scarcely noticed it. In an instant, however, von Brunderger was composed again.

"I go but to see the big ditch before the water is let in," he replied. "And since your gun is to have a test I shall be glad to witness that. You see, I am commissioned by my Kaiser to learn all that you Americans will allow me to in reference to your ways of doing things—in the army, the navy and in the pursuit of peace. After all, preparation for war is the best means of securing peace. Your officers have been more than kind and I have taken advantage

98

of the offer to go to Panama. Lieutenant Blake said the ship would stop here, and, as I had business in Cuba, I came and waited. I am delighted to see you both again."

He went below, leaving Tom and Ned staring at one another.

"Well, what do you think of it?" asked Ned.

"I don't see anything to be worried about," declared Tom. "It's true that a German once tried to make trouble for me, but this von Brunderger is all right, as far as I can learn. He has the highest references, and is an accredited representative of the Kaiser. You are too suspicious, Ned, just as you were in the case of General Waller."

"Maybe so."

From Santiago, swinging around the island of Jamaica, the warship took her way, with the big gun, to Colon. When half way across the Caribbean Sea they encountered rough weather.

The storm broke without any unusual preliminaries, but quickly increased to a hurricane, and when night fell it saw the big ship rolling and tossing in a tempestuous sea. Tom was anxious about his big gun, but the captain assured him that double lashings would make it perfectly safe.

Tom and Ned had seen little of the German officer that day, nor, in fact, since he came aboard. He kept much in the quarters of the other officers, and the report was current that he was a "jolly good fellow."

Rather anxious as to the outcome of the storm, Tom turned in late that night, not expecting to sleep much, for there were many unusual noises. But he did drop off into a doze, only to be awakened about an hour later by a commotion on deck.

"What's up, Ned?" he called to his chum, who had an adjoining stateroom.

"I don't know, Tom. Something is going on, though. Hear that thumping and pounding!"

As Ned spoke there came a tremendous noise from the deck.

"By Jove!" yelled Tom, jumping from his berth. "It's my big gun! It has torn loose from the lashings and may roll overboard!"

CHAPTER XXII

AT GATUN LOCKS

"Steady there now, men! Pass forward those lashings! Careful! Look out, or you'll be caught by it when she rolls! Another turn around the bitts!"

It was the officer of the deck giving orders to a number of marines and sailors as Tom hastily clad, leaped on deck, followed by his chum. The warship was pitching and tossing worse than ever in the heaving billows, and the men were engaged in making fast the giant cannon, which, as Tom had surmised, had torn loose from the steel cables holding it down on deck.

"Come on, Ned!" cried Tom. "We've got to help here!"

"That's right. Look at her swing, would you? If she hits anything it's a goner!"

The breech of the gun appeared to be the end that had come loose, while the muzzle still held fast. And this immense mass of steel was swinging about, eluding the efforts of the ship's officers and crew to capture it. And it seemed only a question of time when the muzzle would tear loose, too. Then, free on deck, the giant cannon would roll through the frail bulwarks, and plunge into the depths of the sea.

"Look out for yourselves, boys!" cried the officer, as he saw Tom and Ned. "This is no plaything!"

"I know it!" gasped Tom. "But we've got to fasten it down."

"That's what we're trying to do," answered the other. "We did get the bight of a cable over the breech, but the men could not hold it, even though they took a couple of turns around the bitts."

"Ned, go call Koku!" cried Tom. "We need him up here."

"That's right!" declared his chum. "If anyone can hold the cable with the weight of the big gun straining on it, the giant can. I'll get him!"

"On deck, Koku, quick!" gasped Ned. "Master's cannon may fall into the sea."

"But the powder!" asked the big man, simply. "Master told me to guard the powder. I stay here."

"No, I'll stay!" insisted Ned. "You are needed on deck, I'll take your place here."

Koku stared uncomprehendingly for a moment, while the loosened gun continued to thump and pound on the deck as though it would burst

100

through. Then it filtered through the dull brain of honest Koku what was wanted.

"I go," he said, and he hurried up the companionway, while Ned, eager to be with Tom, took up the less exciting work of guarding the powder.

Once more, with the giant strength of Koku to aid in the work, the task of lashing the gun again to the deck was undertaken. A bight of steel cable was gotten around the breech, and then passed to a big bitt, or stanchion, bolted to the deck. Koku, working on the heaving deck, amid the hurricane, took a turn around the brace.

There came a roll of the ship that threatened to send the gun sliding against the stanchion, but Koku braced himself. His arms, great bunches of muscles, strained and fairly cracked with the strain. The wire rope seemed to give. Then, as the ship rolled the other way, the strain eased. Koku, aided by the cable, and by the leverage given by the several turns about the bitts, had held the big gun.

"Quick!" cried Tom. "Now another rope so it can't roll the opposite way, and we'll have her."

For a moment the ship was on a level keel, and taking advantage of this, when the weight of the gun would be neutral, another cable was passed around it. Then it was a comparatively easy matter to put on more lashings until the giant cannon was once more fast.

"Whew! But that was tough work!" exclaimed Tom, as he once more entered the stateroom with Ned.

"It must have been," agreed his chum, who had been relieved at the powder station by the giant.

"I thought it would surely go overboard," went on Tom. "Only for Koku it would have. Those fellows couldn't hold it when the ship rolled."

"How did it happen to get loose?" asked Ned.

"Oh, the cables frayed, I suppose. I'll take a look in the morning. Say, but this is some storm!"

"Is the gun all right now?"

"Yes, it's fastened down like a mummy. It can't get loose unless the whole deck comes with it. We can sleep in peace."

"Not much sleep in this blow, I guess," responded Ned.

But they did manage to get some rest by morning, at which time the hurricane seemed to have blown itself out. The day saw the sea gradually

101

calm down, and the big cannon was made additionally secure against a possible recurrence of the accident. But a few days more and it would be safe at Colon.

Tom and Ned had gone on deck soon after breakfast to look at the cannon. All about were pieces of the broken cables, that had been cast aside when the new lashings were put on. Ned picked up one end, remarking:

"These seem mighty strong. It's queer how they broke."

"Well, there was quite a weight upon them," spoke Tom.

Ned did not reply for a moment. Then, as he looked at another piece of a severed cable, he exclaimed:

"Tom, the weight of your gun never broke these."

"What do you mean, Ned?"

"I mean that they were partly filed, or cut through—then the storm and the pressure of the gun did the rest. Look!"

He held out the piece of wire rope. There, on the end, could be seen several strands cleanly severed, as though a file or a hacksaw had been used.

"By Jove!" murmured Tom. He looked about the deck. There was no one near the big gun. "Ned," whispered his chum, "there's something wrong here. It's more of that conspiracy to defeat my aims. Don't say anything about this, and we'll keep our eyes open. We'll do a bit of detective work."

"The scoundrels!" exclaimed Ned. "I wish we knew who they were. General Waller isn't aboard, and what other of the officers has a gun of his own that he would rather see accepted by the government than yours?"

"None that I know of," replied Tom.

"General Waller might have hired someone to—"

"Don't go making any unwarranted charges," warned the young inventor.

"Or perhaps that German, Tom, might—"

"Hush!" cautioned Tom. "Here he comes now," and, as he spoke, General von Brunderger came strolling along the deck.

"I am glad to see that the accident of last night had no serious effects," he said, smiling.

"It was no accident!" burst out Ned.

"No accident? You surprise me. I thought—"

"Oh, Ned means that some of the cables look as though they had been cut," hastily put in Tom, nudging his chum in the ribs as a signal for him to keep quiet.

"The cables cut!" exclaimed the German, and his voice indicated anxious solicitude.

"Or else filed," went on Tom easily, with a warning glance at Ned. "But I dare say they were old cables, that had been used on other work, and may have become frayed. Everything is safe now, though. New cables were lashed on this morning."

"I am glad to hear it. It would be a—er—ah, a national calamity to lose so valuable a gun, and the opening of the canal so near at hand. I am glad that your invention is safe, Herr Swift," and he smiled genially at Tom and Ned.

"What did you shut me off for?" asked Ned, when he and his chum were alone in their stateroom again.

"Because I didn't want you to make any breaks before him," answered Tom.

"Then you suspect—"

"I suspect many things, Ned, but I'm not going to show my hand until I'm ready. I'm going to watch and listen."

"And I'll be with you."

But no further accidents occurred. There were no more storms, no attempt was made to meddle with Tom's powder, and in due season the ship arrived at Colon, and after much labor the great gun, its carriage, the shells and the powder were taken to the barbette at the Gatun locks, designed to admit vessels from the Caribbean Sea into Gatun Lake.

"And now for some more hard work," remarked Tom, as all the needful stores were landed.

CHAPTER XXIII

NEWS OF THE MINE

"Just a little farther over this way, Ned. That's better. Now mark it there, and we'll have it clamped down."

"But can you get enough elevation here, Tom?"

"Oh, yes, I think so. Besides, I've added a few more inches to the lift of the disappearing carriage, and it will send the gun so much farther in the air. I think this will do. Where is Koku?"

"Here I be, Master."

"Just get hold of that small derrick, Koku, and lift up one of the projectiles. I want to see if they come in the right place for the breech before I set the hoisting apparatus permanently."

The giant was soon engaged in winding up the rope of an improvised hoist that stood about in the position the permanent one was to go. From the interior of the barbette, which was, in effect, a bomb-proof structure, there was lifted one of the big projectiles destined to be hurled from Tom Swift's giant cannon.

"Yes, I think that will do," decided the young inventor, as he watched Koku. "Now, Mr. Damon, if you will kindly oversee this part of the work, I'll see if we can't get that motor in better shape. It didn't work worth a cent this morning."

"Bless my rubber coat, Tom, I'll do all I can to help you!" declared the odd man.

"Massa Tom! Massa Tom!" called Eradicate.

"Yes, Rad. What is it?"

"Heah am dem chicken sandwiches, an' some hot coffee fo' yo' all. I done knowed yo' all wouldn't hab no time t' stop fo' dinnah, so I done made yo' all up a snack."

"That's mighty good of you, Rad," spoke Tom, with a laugh. "I was getting pretty hungry; but I didn't want to stop until I had things moving in better shape. Come on, Ned, let's knock off for a few minutes and take a bite. You, too, Mr. Damon."

As they sat about the place where the gun was being mounted, munching sandwiches and drinking the coffee which the aged colored man had so thoughtfully provided, Eradicate said, with a chuckle:

"By gar! Dey can't git erlong wifout dish yeah coon, arter all! Ha! ha! Dat cocoanut giant he mighty good when it comes t' fastening big guns down so dey won't blow away, but when it comes t' eatin' dey has t' depend on ole Eradicate! Ha! ha! I'se got dat cocoanut giant beat all right!"

"He sure is jealous of Koku," remarked Ned, as Tom and Mr. Damon smiled at the colored man.

"He certainly hit me in the right spot," declared Tom, as he reached for another sandwich.

They had landed from the warship several days before, and from then on there had been hard work and plenty of it. Tom was here, there and everywhere, directing matters so that his gun would be favorably placed.

Some preliminary work had been done before they arrived in the way of preparing a place to mount the gun, and this work was now proceeding. The officers of the ordnance department were in actual charge, but they always deferred to Tom, since he had most at stake.

"It will be some days before you can actually fire your gun; will it not?" asked Ned of his chum, as they finished the lunch, and prepared to resume work.

"Yes—a week at least, I expect. It is taking longer to set up the carriage than I thought. But it will be an improvement over the solid one we formerly used. That was fine, Rad," he concluded as the colored man went back to the shack of which he had taken possession for himself and his cooking operations. It adjoined the quarters to which Tom, Ned, Mr. Damon and Koku had been assigned.

"Golly! I ain't so old yit but what I knows de stuff Massa Tom laiks!" exclaimed the colored man, moving off with a chuckle.

Tom, though he had many suspicions about the cut cables that had nearly been the cause of his gun sliding into the sea, had learned nothing definite—nor had Ned.

The German officer, with his body servant, who seldom spoke, had landed at Colon, and was proceeding to make himself at home with the officers and men who were building the canal. Occasionally he paid a visit to Tom and Ned, where they were engaged about the big gun. He always seemed pleasant, and interested in their labors, asking many question, but that was all, and our hero began to feel that perhaps he was wrong in his suspicions.

As for Ned, he veered uncertainly from one suspicion to another. At one time he declared that von Brunderger and General Waller were in a conspiracy to upset Tom's plans. Again he would accuse the German alone, until Tom laughingly bade him attend more to work and less to theories.

Slowly the work progressed. The gun was mounted after much labor, and then arrangements began to be made for the test. A series of shots were to be fired out to sea, and the proper precautions were to be taken to prevent any ships from being struck.

"Though if you intend to send a projectile thirty miles," said one of the officers, "I'm afraid there may be some danger, after all. Are you sure you have a range of thirty miles, Mr. Swift?"

"I have," answered Tom, calmly, "and with the increased elevation that I am able to get here, it may exceed that."

The officer said nothing, but he looked at Tom in what our hero thought was a peculiar manner.

A few days before the date set for the test one of the sentinels, who had been detailed to keep curiosity-seekers away from the giant cannon, approached Tom and said:

"There is a gentleman asking to see you, Mr. Swift."

"Who is it?" asked Tom, laying aside a pressure gauge he intended attaching to the gun.

"He says his name is Peterson—Alec Peterson. Do you want to see him?"

"Yes, let him come up," directed the young inventor. "Do you hear that, Ned?" he called. "Our fortune-hunting friend is here."

"Maybe he's found that lost opal mine," suggested Ned.

"I hope he has, for dad's sake," went on Tom. "Hello, Mr. Peterson!" he called, as he noticed the old prospector coming along. "Have you had any luck?"

"I heard you were down here," said the man not answering the question directly, "and as I had to run over from my island for some supplies I thought I'd stop and see you. How are you?" and he shook hands.

"Fine!" answered Tom. "Have you found the lost mine yet?"

Alec Peterson paused a moment. Then he said slowly:

"No, Tom, I haven't succeeded in locating the mine yet. But I—I expect to any day now!" he added, hastily.

CHAPTER XXIV

THE LONGEST SHOT

"Well, Mr. Peterson," remarked Tom, after a pause, "I'm sure I hope you will succeed in your quest. You must have met disappointment so far."

"I have, Tom. But I'm not going to give up. Can't you come over and see me before you go back North?"

"I'll try. Just where is your island?"

"Off in that direction," responded the fortune-hunter, pointing to the northeast. "It's a little farther from here than I thought it was at first—about thirty miles. But I have a little second-hand steam launch that my pardners and I use. I'll come for you, take you over and bring you back any time you say."

"After my gun has been tested," said Tom, with a smile. "Better stay and see it."

"No, I must get back to the island. I have some new information that I am sure will enable me to locate the lost mine."

"Well, good-bye, and good luck to you," called Tom, as the fortune-hunter started away.

"Do you think he'll ever find the opals, Tom?" asked Ned.

His chum shook his head.

"I don't believe so," he answered. "Alec has always been that way—always visionary—always just about to be successful; but never quite getting there."

"Then your father's ten thousand dollars will be lost?"

"Yes, I suppose so; but, in a way, dad can stand it. And if I make good on this gun test, ten thousand dollars won't look very big to me. I guess dad gave it to Alec from a sort of sentimental feeling, anyhow."

"You mean because he saved you from the live wire?"

"That's it, Ned. It was a sort of reward, in a way, and I guess dad won't be broken-hearted if Alec doesn't succeed. Only, of course, he'll feel badly for Alec himself. Poor old man! he won't be able to do much more prospecting. Well, Ned, let's get to work on that ammunition hoist. It still jams a little on the ways, and I want it to work smoothly. There's no use having a hitch— even a small one—when the big bugs assemble to see how my cannon shoots."

"That's right, Tom. Well, start off, I'm with you."

The two youths labored for some time, being helped, of course, by the workmen provided by the government, and some from the steel concern.

There were many little details to look after, not the least of which was the patrolling of the stretch of ocean over which the great projectiles would soar in reaching the far-off targets at which Tom had planned to shoot. No ships were to be allowed to cross the thirty-mile mark while the firing was in progress. So, also, the zone where the shots were expected to fall was to be cleared.

But at last all seemed in readiness. The gun had been tried again and again on its carriage. The projectiles were all in readiness, and the terribly powerful ammunition had been stored below the gun in a bomb-proof chamber, ready to be hoisted out as needed.

Because the gun had been fired so many times with a charge of powder heavier than was ordinarily called for, and had stood the strain well, Tom had no fear of standing reasonably close to it to press the button of the battery. There would be no retreating to the bombproof this time.

The German officer was occasionally seen about the place where the gun was mounted, but he appeared to take only an ordinary interest in it. Tom began to feel more than ever that perhaps his suspicions were unfounded.

Some officials high in government affairs had arrived at Colon in anticipation of the test, which, to Tom's delight, had attracted more attention than he anticipated. At the same time he was a bit nervous.

"Suppose it fails, Ned?" he said.

"Oh, it can't!" cried his chum. "Don't think about such a thing."

Plans had been made for a ship to be stationed near the zone of fire, to report by wireless the character of each shot, the distance it traveled, and how near it came to the target. The messages would be received at a station near the barbette, and at once reported to Tom, so that he would know how the test was progressing.

"Well, today tells the tale!" exclaimed the young inventor, as he got up one morning. "How's the weather, Ned?"

"Couldn't be better—clear as a bell, Tom."

"That's good. Well, let's have grub, and then go out and see how my pet is."

"Oh, I guess nothing could happen, with Koku on guard."

"No, hardly. I'm going to keep him in the ammunition room until after the test, too. I'm going to take no chances."

"That's the ticket!"

The gun was found all right, in its great tarpaulin cover, and Tom had the latter taken off that he might go over every bit of mechanism. He made a few slight changes, and then got ready for the final trials.

On an improvised platform, not too near the giant cannon, had gathered the ordnance board, the specially invited guests, a number of officers and workers in the canal zone, and one or two representatives of foreign governments. Von Brunderger was there, but his "familiar," as Ned had come to call the stolid German servant, was not present.

Tom took some little time to explain, modestly enough, the working of his gun. A number of questions were asked, and then it was announced that the first shot, with only a practice charge of powder, would be fired.

"Careful with that projectile now. That's it, slip it in carefully. A little farther forward. That's better. Now the powder—Koku, are you down there?" and Tom called down the tube into the ammunition chamber.

"Me here, Master," was the reply.

"All right, send up a practice load."

Slowly the powerful explosive came up on the electric hoist. It was placed in the firing chamber and the breech dosed.

"Now, gentlemen," said Tom, "this is not a shot for distance. It is merely to try the gun and get it warmed up, so to speak, for the real tests that will follow. All ready?"

"All ready!" answered Ned, who was acting as chief assistant.

"Here she goes!" cried Tom, and he pressed the button.

Many were astonished by the great report, but Tom and the others, who were used to the service charges, hardly noticed this one. Yet when the wireless report came in, giving the range as over fourteen thousand yards, there was a gasp of surprise.

"Over eight miles!" declared one grizzled officer; "and that with only a practice charge. What will happen when he puts in a full one?'

"I don't know," answered a friend.

Tom soon showed them. Quickly he called for another projectile, and it was inserted in the gun. Then the powder began to come up the hoist. Meanwhile the young inventor had assured himself that the gun was all right. Not a part had been strained.

This time, when Tom pressed the button there was such a tremendous concussion that several, who were not prepared for it, were knocked back against their neighbors or sent toppling off their chairs or benches. And as for the report, it was so deafening that for a long time after it many could not hear well.

But Tom, and those who knew the awful power of the big cannon, wore specially prepared eardrum protectors, that served to reduce the shock.

"What is it?" called Tom to the wireless operator, who was receiving the range distance from the marking ship.

"A little less than twenty-nine miles."

"We must do better than that," said Tom. "I'll use more powder, and try one of the newer shells. I'll elevate the gun a trifle, too."

Again came that terrific report, that trembling of the ground, that concussion, that blast of air as it rushed in to fill the vacuum caused, and then the vibrating echoes.

"I think you must have gone the limit this time, Tom!" yelled Ned, as he turned on the compressed air to blow the powder fumes and unconsumed bits of explosive from the gun tube.

"Possibly," admitted Tom. "Here comes the report." The wireless operator waved a slip of paper.

"Thirty-one miles!" he announced.

"Hurray!" cried Mr. Damon. "Bless my telescope! The longest shot on record!"

"I believe it is," admitted the chief of the ordnance department. "I congratulate you, Mr. Swift."

"I think I can do better than that," declared Tom, after looking at the various recording gauges, and noting the elevation of the gun. "I think I can get a little flatter trajectory, and that will give a greater distance. I'm going to try."

"Does that mean more powder, Tom?" asked Ned.

"Yes, and the heaviest shell we have—the one with the bursting charge. I'll fire that, and see what happens. Tell the zone-ship to be on the lookout," he said to the wireless operator, giving a brief statement of what he was about to attempt.

"Isn't it a risk, Tom?" his chum asked.

"Well, not so much. I'm sure my cannon will stand it. Come on now, help me depress the muzzle just a trifle," and by means of the electric current the big gun was raised at the breech a few inches.

As is well known, cannon shots do not go in straight lines. They leave the muzzle, curve upward and come down on another curve. It is this curve described by the projectile that is called the trajectory. The upward curve, as you all know, is caused by the force of the powder, and the downward by the force of gravitation acting on the shot as soon as it reaches its zenith. Were it not for this force the projectiles could be fired in straight lines. But, as it is, the cannon has to be elevated to send the shot up a bit, or it would fall short of its mark.

Consequently, the flatter the trajectory the farther it will go. Tom's object, then, was to flatten the trajectory, by lowering the muzzle of the gun, in order to attain greater distance.

"If this doesn't do the trick, we'll try it with the muzzle a bit lower, and with a trifle more powder," he said to Ned, as he was about to fire.

The young inventor was not a little nervous as he prepared to press the button this time. It was a heavier charge than any used that day, though the same quantity had been fired on other occasions with safety. But he was not going to hesitate.

Coincident with the pressure of Tom's fingers there seemed to be a veritable earthquake. The ground swayed and rocked, and a number of the spectators staggered back. It was like the blast of a hundred thunderbolts. The gun shook as it recoiled from the shock, but the wonderful disappearing carriage, fitted with coiled, pneumatic and hydrostatic buffers, stood the strain.

Following the awful report, the terrific recoil and the howl of the wind as it rushed into the vacuum created, there was an intense silence. The projectile had been seen by some as a dark speck, rushing through the air like a meteor. Then the wireless operator could be seen writing down a message, the telephone-like receivers clamped over his ears.

"Something happened, all right!" he called aloud. "That shot hit something."

"Not one of the ships!" cried Tom, aghast.

"I don't know. There seems to be some difficulty in transmitting. Wait—I'm getting it: now."

As he ceased speaking there came from underneath the great gun the sound of confused shouts. Tom and Ned recognized Koku's voice protesting:

"No—no—you can't come in here! Master said no one was to come in."

"What is it, Koku?" yelled Tom, springing to the speaking tube connecting with the powder magazine, at the same time keeping an eye on the wireless operator. Tom was torn between two anxieties.

"Someone here, Master!" cried the giant. "Him try to fix powder. Ah, I fix you!" and with a savage snarl the giant, in the concrete chamber below, could be heard to attack someone who cried out gutturally in German:

"Help! Help! Help!"

"Come on, Ned!" cried Tom, making a dash for the stairs that led into the magazine. There was confusion all about, but through it all the wireless operator continued to write down the message coming to him through space.

"What is it, Koku? What is it?" cried Tom, plunging down into the little chamber.

As he reached it, a door leading to the outer air flew open, and out rushed a man, badly torn as to his clothes, and scratched and bleeding as to his face. On he ran, across the space back of the barbette, toward the lower tier of seats that had been erected for the spectators.

"It's von Brunderger's servant!" gasped Ned, recognizing the fellow.

"What did he do, Koku?" demanded the young inventor.

"Him sneak in here—have some of that stuff you call 'dope.' I sent up powder, and I come back here to see him try to put some dope in Master's ammunition."

"The scoundrel!" cried Tom. "They're trying to break me, even at the last minute! Come on, Ned."

They raced outside to behold a curious sight. Straight toward von Brunderger rushed the man as if in a frenzy of fear. He called out something in German to his master, and the latter's face went first red, then white. He was observed to look about quickly, as though in alarm, and then, with a shout at his servant, the German officer rushed from the stand, and the two disappeared in the direction of the barracks.

"What does it mean?" cried Ned.

"Give it up," answered Tom, "except that Koku spoiled their trick, whatever it was. It looks as if this was the end of it, and that the mystery has been cleared up."

"Mr. Swift! Where's Mr. Swift?" shouted the wireless operator. "Where are you?"

"Yes; what is it?" demanded Tom, so excited that he hardly knew what he was doing.

"The longest shot on record!" cried the man. "Thirty-three miles, and it struck, exploded, and blew the top off a mountain on an island out there!" and he pointed across the sun-lit sea.

CHAPTER XXV

THE LONG-LOST MINE

There was a silence after the inspiring words of the operator, and then it seemed that everyone began to talk at once. The record-breaking shot, the effect of it and the struggle that had taken place in the powder room, together with the flight of von Brunderger and his servant, gave many subjects for excited conversation.

"I've got to get at the bottom of this!" cried Tom, making his way through the press of officials to where the wireless operator stood. "Just repeat that," requested Tom, and they all gave place for him, waiting for the answer.

The operator read the message again.

"Thirty-three miles!" murmured Tom. "That is better than I dared to hope. But what's that about blowing the top off an island?"

"That's what you did, with that explosive shell, Mr. Swift. The operator on the firing-zone ship saw the top fly off when the shell struck. The ship was about half a mile away, and when they heard that shell coming the officers thought it was all up with them. But, instead, it passed over them and demolished the top of the mountain.

"Anybody hurt?" asked Tom, anxiously.

"No, it was an uninhabited island. But you have made the record shot, all right. It went farther than any of the others."

"Then I suppose I ought to be satisfied," remarked Tom, with a smile.

"What was that disturbance, Mr. Swift?" asked the chief ordnance officer, coming forward.

"I don't understand it myself," replied the young inventor. "It appeared that someone went into the ammunition room, and Koku, my giant servant, attacked him."

"As he had a right to do. But who was the intruder?"

"Herr von Brunderger's man."

"Ha! That German officer's! Where is he, he must explain this."

But Herr von Brunderger was not to be found, nor was his man in evidence. They had fled, and when a search was made of their rooms, damaging evidence was found. Before a board of investigating officers Koku told his story, after the gun tests had been declared off for the day, they having been most satisfactory.

The German officer's servant, it appeared, had managed to gain entrance to the ammunition chamber by means of a false key to the outer door. There were two entrances, the other being from the top of the platform where the cannon rested. Koku had seen him about to throw something into one of the ammunition cases, and had grappled with him. There was a fight, and, in spite of the giant's strength, the man had slipped away, leaving part of his garments in the grasp of Koku.

An investigation of some of the powder showed that it had been covered with a chemical that would have made it explode prematurely when placed in the gun. It would probably have wrecked the cannon by blowing out the breech block, and might have done serious damage to life as well as property.

"But what was the object?" asked Ned.

"To destroy Tom's gun," declared Mr. Damon.

"Why should von Brunderger want to do that?"

They found the answer among his papers. He had been a German officer of high rank, but had been dismissed from the secret service of his country for bad conduct. Then, it appeared, he thought of the plan of doing some damage to a foreign country in order to get back in the good graces of his Fatherland.

He forged documents of introduction and authority, and was received with courtesy by the United States officials. In some way he heard of Tom's gun, and that it was likely to be so successful that it would be adopted by the United States government. This he wanted to prevent, and he went to great lengths to accomplish this. It was he, or an agent of his, who forged the letter of invitation to General Waller, and who first tried to spoil Tom's test by doping the powder through Koku.

Later he tried other means, sending a midnight visitor to Tom's house and even going to the length of filing the cables in the storm, so the gun would roll off the warship into the sea. All this was found set down in his papers, for he kept a record of what he had done in order to prove his case to his own government. It was his servant who tried to get near the gun while it was being cast.

That he would be restored to favor had he succeeded, was an open question, though with Germany's friendliness toward the United States it is probable that his acts would have been repudiated. But he was desperate.

Failing in many attempts he resolved on a last one. He sent his servant to the ammunition room to "dope" the powder, hoping that, at the next shot, the gun would be mined. Perhaps he hoped to disable Tom. But the plot failed, and the conspirators escaped. They were never heard of again, probably leaving Panama under assumed names and in disguise.

"Well, that explains the mystery," said Tom to Ned a few days later. "I guess we won't have to worry any more."

"No, and I'm sorry I suspected General Waller."

"Oh, well, he'll never know it, so no harm is done. Oh, but I'm glad this is over. It has gotten on my nerves."

"I should say so," agreed Ned.

"Bless my pillow sham!" cried Mr. Damon. "I think I can get a good night's sleep now. So they have formally accepted your giant cannon, Tom?"

"Yes. The last tests I gave them, showing how easily it could be manipulated, convinced them. It will be one of the official defense guns of the Panama Canal."

"Good! I congratulate you, my boy!" cried the odd man. "And now, bless my postage stamp, let's get back to the United States."

"Before we go," suggested Ned, "let's go take a look at that island from which Tom blew the top. It must be quite a sight—and thirty-three miles away! We can get a launch and go out."

But there was no need. That same day Alec Peterson came to Colon inquiring for Tom. His face showed a new delight.

"Why," cried Tom, "you look as though you had found your opal mine."

"I have!" exclaimed the fortune-hunter. "Or, rather, Tom, I think I have you to thank for finding it for me."

"Me find it?"

"Yes. Did you hear about the top of the island-mountain you blew to pieces?"

"We did, but—"

"That was my island!" exclaimed Mr. Peterson. "The mine was in that mountain, but an earthquake had covered it. I should never have found it but for you. That shot you accidentally fired ripped the mountain apart. My men and I were fortunately at the base of it then, but we sure thought our time had come when that shell struck. It went right over our heads. But it did the business, all right, and opened up the old mine. Tom, your father won't lose his money, we'll all be rich. Oh, that was a lucky shot! I knew it was your cannon that did it."

"I'm glad of it!" answered the young inventor, heartily. "Glad for your sake, Mr. Peterson."

"You must come and see the mine—your mine, Tom, for it never would have been rediscovered had it not been for your giant cannon, that made the longest shot on record, so I'm told."

"We will come, Mr. Peterson, just as soon as I close up matters here."

It did not take Tom long to do this. His type of cannon was formally accepted as a defense for the Panama Canal, and he received a fine contract to allow that type to be used by the government. His powder and projectiles, too, were adopted.

Then, one day, he and Ned, with Koku and Mr. Damon, visited the scene of

home. "I'm going to take a long rest, and the only thing I'm going to invent for the next six months is a new potato slicer." But whether Tom kept his words can be learned by reading the next volume of this series.

"Bless my hand towel!" cried Mr. Damon. "I think you are entitled to a rest, Tom."

"That's what I say," agreed Ned.

"I'll take care ob him—I'll take care ob Massa Tom," put in Eradicate, as he cast a quick look at Koku. "Giants am all right fo' cannon wuk, but when it comes t' comforts Massa Tom gwine t' 'pend on ole 'Radicate; ain't yo' all, Massa Tom?"

"I guess so, Rad!" exclaimed the young inventor, with a laugh. "Is dinner ready?"

"It suah am, Massa Tom, an' I 'specially made some oh dat fricasseed chicken yo' all does admire so much. Plenty of it, too, Massa Tom."

"That's good, Rad," put in Ned. "For we'll all be hungry after that trip to the island. That sure was a great shot Tom—thirty-three miles!"

"Yes, it went farther than I thought it would," replied Tom. And now, as they are taking a closing meal at Panama, ready to return to the United States, we will take leave of Tom Swift and his friends.

Milton Keynes UK
Ingram Content Group UK Ltd.
UKHW040736030823
426269UK00004B/271